THE RULES
OF HIS
BABY BARGAIN

THE RULES
OF HIS
BABY BARGAIN

LOUISE FULLER

MILLS & BOON

First published in Great Britain 2020
by Mills & Boon, an imprint of HarperCollins*Publishers*
1 London Bridge Street, London, SE1 9GF

www.harpercollins.co.uk

HarperCollins*Publishers*
1st Floor, Watermarque Building, Ringsend Road
Dublin 4, Ireland

Large Print edition 2021

© 2020 Louise Fuller

ISBN: 978-0-263-28832-2

MIX
Paper from
responsible sources
FSC™ C007454

This book is produced from independently certified FSC™ paper to ensure responsible forest management. For more information visit www.harpercollins.co.uk/green.

Printed and bound in Great Britain
by CPI Group (UK) Ltd, Croydon, CR0 4YY

To Alison Porter.
For staying so sane and strong
among the crazies!
Thank you for being such a good friend.
Twenty-eight years and counting. X

CHAPTER ONE

Umbrella in hand, Dora Thorn stopped walking and gazed up at the number on the imposing black door, her heart pounding in time to the raindrops hitting the glistening London pavement.

With fingers that trembled slightly she pulled out her earbuds, her choppy blonde hair flopping in front of her eyes as she turned her head and glanced back down the street.

This must be it.

Reaching into her bag, she pulled out the letter, scanning the address even though she had read it a hundred times already on the bus journey over.

120 Gresham Street

Her eyes darted back up to the number, her pulse beating out of time, and then she saw it. Tucked away, barely visible in the dull March light, was a discreet brass plate that said *Capel Muir Fellowes.*

This was definitely the place.

She took a breath, pressed the buzzer beneath the nameplate, and waited for a heartbeat as the door clicked open.

Pushing aside a rush of nerves, and the feeling that at any moment she was going to be asked to leave, she walked swiftly across a polished concrete floor towards the two young men sitting behind an elegant reception desk.

As she stopped in front of the one nearest to her, he looked up and smiled. Not quite a come-on—he was clearly too professional for that—but there was a definite glint in his eye—

'May I help you?'

'I hope so.' Dora hesitated, then smiled back.

For the last seven weeks the only male in her life had been one who wore nappies and only had eight teeth, and she had actually forgotten that adult men could look attractive. And clean. Archie was always so sticky, particularly now that he wanted to feed himself.

Before—before everything had changed—she would have flirted. She might even have fallen in love, and then out of love just as quickly. After all, life was for living. Or that was what she'd used to think.

Her shoulders tensed, bracing her against a wave of misery.

'My name is Dora Thorn and I have a meeting with—' she frowned and, shifting her umbrella beneath her arm, glanced down at the letter '—with Mr Muir.'

She stared at the man in front of her, confused, when his eyes widened with a mixture of shock and panic. Beside him, his colleague glanced up at her furtively.

'Of course. I'll get him right away. Would you like to take a seat, Ms Thorn?'

Nodding, she made her way over to a group of expensive-looking armchairs, and sat down, feeling a queasy mix of relief and sadness.

Over the last few weeks there had been so many letters and emails from people she didn't know or had never met, and then finally, three days ago, there had been a name she'd recognised.

Capel Muir Fellowes were her father's lawyers—or at least they had been. And she'd had a missed call from him on her phone the evening before the letter had arrived.

Dora felt her chest tighten. She hadn't seen

or heard from her father since Della's funeral. Given his track record, she hadn't really expected him to stay in touch, and it was hard to give him credit for reaching out now.

But maybe losing one daughter had reminded David Thorn that he was still the parent of another.

Her mouth twisted. *Doubtful.*

More likely he felt some kind of responsibility for his grandson. Financial responsibility anyway. He'd opted out of hands-on parenting a long time ago.

Of course it was just a hunch. David, being David, hadn't left a message to tell her any of this himself. But getting some third party to deal with her was just his style, and logically it was the only explanation.

She breathed out softly. After all, why else would his lawyers—or any lawyers, for that matter—get in touch?

It wasn't as if there was anything left to take away from her.

Her throat tightened, and she swallowed against the pain that had not been blunted by the seven weeks that had passed since that appalling morning when two police officers had turned up on her doorstep.

She'd only just gone to bed, and she'd been dazed and stupid with lack of sleep, her head still spinning with one too many tequila shots. She'd assumed that she must have done something stupid the night before.

Because it would have had to be about *her*, of course.

Not for a moment had it occurred to her that the police might want to talk to her about Della. But then, why would they have?

Della had always been the perfect big sister. A bit bossy, but conscientious, kind, hard-working and always so very, very sensible. The sort of person who waited for the green man before crossing the road and even then would look both ways—*twice*.

It just hadn't seemed possible that anything could happen to her.

But it had.

Impossibly, devastatingly, her wonderful, brave, stoic sister had been knocked off her bike on the way to work. She had been pronounced dead on arrival at the hospital.

Dora felt tears jump into her eyes.

In the few seconds it had taken for the police officer to say those words everything had been sucked out of her. She had known she was still alive, but her life had changed for ever, broken into a million tiny, irretrievable pieces.

She felt her muscles tense as the memory of that morning crept back into her head.

Losing Della had been like losing a limb—a sharp, searing pain, followed by a dull ache that just wouldn't fade. Dora hadn't been able to see, much less speak to anyone, for fear of breaking down. Her heart had felt like a stone. All she'd wanted to do was crawl into bed and hide away from everyone—hide from a world where something so terrible and unfair could strike at random.

And if it had been just her, that was exactly what she would have done.

But she'd had to take care of Archie.

Her heart contracted. If the shock of losing her sister had been like hitting an iceberg head-on, then the realisation that she was in charge of bringing up her eleven-month-old nephew had been like trying to navigate an endless sea without a compass.

She loved him so much it hurt—but it terrified her too, being a grown-up. There was so much to sort out and learn—and not just day-to-day baby stuff.

Della had left no will.

Dora's throat tightened sharply. That was only the second time in her life that her uber-organised, efficient sister had acted out of character.

The first time—more improbable by far—had been just under two years ago, when Della had fallen in love with the billionaire gambling tycoon Lao Dan.

Lao Dan had been more than twice her age.

He had also been her boss.

And Della hadn't just fallen in love. She had got pregnant too. With Archie.

Letting out a breath, Dora dragged her thoughts back to the present.

Leaving no will—or dying intestate, as she now knew it to be called—didn't just mean that her sister hadn't left any instructions for how she wanted everything to work on her death. It also introduced a layer of complication and a mind-blowing amount of paperwork to an already fraught situation. Dora even had to apply to become Archie's guardian.

Her stomach tensed and she stared down at her hands, guilt momentarily swamping her.

Would she have acted the same way if Della had actually appointed her in her will? Or was she just looking for an excuse?

'Ms Thorn?'

Standing in front of her was a middle-aged man in a dark pinstriped suit, his silvery hair gleaming only slightly less than his teeth. Grateful to change the path of her thoughts, she stood up.

'What a pleasure to meet you—and thank you so much for coming in today. I'm Peter Muir, one of the senior partners.' He took Dora's hand, and shook it briskly. 'And on behalf of the firm I'd like to offer our sincere condolences for your loss. Such a terrible accident.'

She felt her smile freeze over as his hand squeezed hers sympathetically.

'Thank you,' she said quickly. She didn't want or need comfort from a stranger, but in some ways it was a relief to know that her hunch had been right. Clearly her father was behind this. How else would this lawyer know the details of Della's death?

Ignoring the curious glances of the receptionists, she let Peter Muir guide her towards a sweeping staircase at the end of the hallway.

'I thought we'd use the partners' lounge. It's a little cosier than my office.' His face creased apologetically. 'I'm afraid Mr Law is running a little late, but he's on his way and should be with us very soon.'

Dora nodded politely, hoping her own face wasn't betraying her ignorance and confusion. Since she had no idea who Mr Law was, his lateness was immaterial to her. But clearly she wasn't about to tell Mr Muir that.

'Here we are.'

She blinked. Clearly he had a very different idea of 'cosy' from hers. The room was larger than the whole of her downstairs at home, with huge bay windows and a selection of comfortable sofas and armchairs. Above the period fireplace a huge rectangular mirror ran the entire length of one wall.

'Would you like some refreshments? Coffee, tea…?'

Thanks to Archie's molars, she had overslept and hadn't actually had time to eat or drink anything that morning. What she really wanted was a couple of Danish pastries.

'Coffee would be lovely,' she said quickly. 'Milk, no sugar, please.'

'Ah, Susannah.' Mr Muir turned as a glacially beautiful blonde straight out of a Hitchcock movie appeared in the doorway, one perfect eyebrow raised in anticipation.

'Some coffee for Ms Thorn, please. If you'll

excuse me a moment, Ms Thorn, I'll get the paperwork.'

'Of course.'

Left alone, she sank back into a smooth velvet-covered sofa and then instantly sat up straight. If she started to relax she would to fall asleep. She needed to stay alert, to concentrate.

With Della gone, she was the grown-up. And if that wasn't terrifying enough to keep her awake, she wasn't just responsible for herself, but for Archie too.

It made her feel young and frightened, and yet her sister had made it look so effortless—not just with Archie, but after she'd been left to raise Dora after their father had left.

Remembering her younger self, Dora grimaced. She had been a typical teenager. Stroppy. Lazy. Always complaining that everything was unfair or boring.

But their home had always been tidy.

There had always been food in the fridge.

And Della had certainly never felt so overwhelmed that she'd looked into putting Dora up for adoption.

The silence in the room was suddenly stifling, and she stared dully at the grey sky outside the window, feeling the guilt she had tried so hard to stifle bubbling up inside her.

She had made that call at the end of last week. After a particularly difficult few days.

Ever since Della's death Archie had been understandably unsettled and clingy, but Dora usually managed to distract him and calm him down. This time, though, nothing she'd done had worked.

He had been inconsolable, red-faced and furious.

Exhausted, desperate and defeated, she had finally been forced to acknowledge what he was clearly feeling and admit what she had known right from the start.

She could never be Della.

She could never replace her sister—his mother.

She was an imposter who could barely take care of herself, much less a baby.

What Archie needed—what he deserved—was to be looked after properly by someone who knew what she was doing.

It had been a relief to make the call the next day, and the woman at the adoption agency had been very kind and calm, not judgemental at all. But even before the interview had been over Dora had known she could never let Archie go.

Yes, life with him was going to be challenging, and time-consuming, and exhausting sometimes. But without him it would be unbearable.

He was her flesh and blood, the last link she had with her sister, and when she'd picked him up from the nursery she had held him close and sworn to do her very best for him, just as her sister had done for her.

Whatever sacrifice needed to be made, she would make it. Even if it meant being a glorified waitress with a smile glued to her face.

Serving cocktails at Blakely's, a casino in the West End, was hardly her dream job, but the tips were good, and right now she couldn't even contemplate looking for something else.

Besides, whatever she did it wouldn't—couldn't—be what she really wanted to do.

But she wasn't going to think about that now, and with relief she watched as Susannah reappeared holding a tray. As well as a pot of coffee, she had brought a plate of biscotti, and as she slid it onto a low table, Dora had to clench her hands in her lap to stop herself from grabbing one and stuffing it into her mouth.

'Thank you. This looks lovely.'

Susannah smiled perfunctorily. 'Mr Muir

asked me to tell you that Mr Law has just arrived and they will be up shortly.'

Dora nodded. This Mr Law must be some kind of senior partner for everyone to be so excited about him.

'It's quite funny if you think about it…being called Law and being a lawyer. It's like being Mr Bun the Baker.'

Stop babbling, she told herself. But the other woman's poise and perfect skin were so intimidating it was making Dora feel nervous all over again.

'I suppose that's why they left his name out when they named the company. I mean, it might confuse people.'

Susannah stared at her, then frowned. 'Mr Law—'

'Is here. Thank you, Susannah.'

Peter Muir strode into the room, smiling broadly. But Dora was still too busy trying to understand the expression on the other woman's face to look properly at the man following him. She'd seemed confused, or astonished, but there was no time to ponder why.

'And this is Ms Thorn.'

Standing up, Dora smiled automatically and

held out her hand, but her smile wavered as the second man took a step towards her.

She felt her jaw slacken. *Breathe*, she told herself as she stared up at him.

Given the reverence surrounding him, she'd been expecting an older man, but he was young, in his mid-thirties at most, and that on its own dazzled her momentarily.

But her surprise was forgotten almost immediately as two thoughts collided in her head. The first was that, quite frankly, he was the most beautiful man she had ever seen in her life. The second, disconcertingly, was that he seemed strangely familiar.

But clearly, judging by his lack of reaction, Charlie Law was not experiencing a similar sense of déjà vu.

Or maybe she was dreaming, she thought. Since Della's death her nights had been full of vivid, confusing dreams that jolted her awake in the darkness.

But this man was real, fiercely controlled and superbly male.

Sleek dark hair, high cheekbones and a subtle curve of a mouth fought for her attention, and heat spilled out slowly over her skin, almost as if she was standing under a warm shower.

Inclining his head slightly to the left, he let his cool dark eyes lock onto hers, and she felt something unravel inside her as his hand curved around hers, his touch sending a jolt of electricity through the tips of her fingers.

His grip was firm, yet not aggressively so. But, aside from mesmerising good looks, he had an air of authority that meant he clearly felt no need to resort to traditional male posturing.

Her insides tightened. She couldn't seem to breathe properly, and her heart was thumping so hard she could feel it hitting her ribs.

It wasn't the first time she had locked eyes with a man. But he was the first man to look at her so intently that it was impossible to look away. It felt as if he was reaching inside her.

Only that wasn't what made a shiver run down her spine. As his dark eyes slowly inspected her from head to toe, she realised with a beat of shock that Charlie Law both desired and disapproved of her.

Her shoulders tensed.

She was familiar with both reactions—just never from the same person at the same time. And she found herself taken aback by his censure. Why would he feel that way about her, a stranger?

She held her breath as his gaze hovered on her face momentarily, and then he turned towards the lawyer. 'Thank you, Peter, I think I can take it from here. That is if Ms Thorn has no objections?'

Dora felt the tension in her shoulders inch down her spine.

It was the first time she had heard him speak and his voice had caught her off balance. It was measured, quiet...the voice of a man who didn't need to shout. The kind of voice that came from knowing everyone was on tenterhooks, waiting to do your bidding.

Aware that her reaction to him was probably written all over her face, she felt a sudden flicker of irritation at his unspoken assumption that she was included in that group.

'Oh, I can probably survive,' she said lightly, wanting him to know that she wasn't intimidated by him.

He didn't reply, just stood watching her, waiting until the door had closed behind Mr Muir before sitting down in one of the armchairs. She was still standing, and he gestured towards the sofa.

'Please, take a seat.'

She sat down again, her heart thudding as his

dark eyes rested on her face, wanting to cross her arms protectively in front of her body but not wanting him to know that she cared what he thought.

'I'm going to have some coffee,' she said abruptly. 'Would you like a cup?'

His expression didn't change.

'I don't drink coffee. In any case, I'd prefer to get down to business. I have another meeting to get to.'

Her eyes narrowed a fraction at his dismissive tone, and it was on the tip of her tongue to ask him why, then, had he arranged to meet with her this morning? But, really, what did it matter to her? What did *he* matter to her? Anyway, her father was the one paying for his time.

'But surely it's not as important as this one. With me,' she added crisply.

His mouth tightened imperceptibly, and she felt it again. That flashbulb moment of recognition. She knew it must be her mind playing tricks on her. And yet...

'I'm sorry,' she said slowly. 'But have we ever met before? It's just you seem really familiar.'

For a moment he continued to stare at her impassively, studying her face, considering her question, considering his answer, and she felt another bite of irritation. Seconds ago he'd told her he had another meeting, but now he apparently had all the time in the world.

'That's probably because I look like my brother,' he said finally.

She felt it first in her stomach—a creeping, icy unease that spread outwards through her limbs and down her spine.

Her chest squeezed tight and she shook her head, wanting to look away. Except she couldn't. She was trapped—caught in his steady, unblinking gaze. 'I don't think I know your brother.'

'Oh, but you do,' he said softly, and now he smiled—except it was the kind of calm, controlled smile that didn't reach his eyes. 'You know him very well.' He paused. 'Your nephew, Archie, is my brother. Half-brother, to be precise.'

The room swam. Her heart stopped beating. Her blood felt as though it had turned to ice. She stared at him, words of denial stuck in her throat, her mouth open in shock.

But of course. Now she knew she could see it. In the shape of his mouth and that flash of anger. It was Archie. He looked like Archie—Della's Archie.

Her Archie.

A knot formed in her stomach. Head spinning, she took a breath, tried to focus her brain, re-playing fragments of conversation, things Della had said.

Archie's father, Lao Dan, had other children—older children—daughters from previous marriages and a son. Charlie.

She swallowed around the lump swelling in her throat.

So that meant Charlie's mother had been Lao Dan's wife when Della had been his mistress. Now, at least, she understood Charlie's disapproval. She still didn't understand why he was here in this room, though. With her.

'You're not a lawyer,' she said flatly.

He shook his head.

She glared at him. 'And you lied about your surname too.'

'I didn't lie. You assumed I was a lawyer. And adopting an English surname is fairly common practice. It stops any awkward mispronunciation.'

An icy heat shivered down her back. 'So what do you want?'

But she knew what he wanted even before he could open his beautiful curving mouth to reply.

'No,' she said, shaking her head as if that

would somehow make her voice stop shaking. 'No,' she repeated. 'Archie is *my* nephew—'

'And *my* brother.'

Suddenly it felt as if everything was moving very slowly, so that his words seemed to take ages to reach her. Panic clawed at her, anger flaring up from nowhere, as it had started to do ever since Della's death.

Her eyes locked with his. 'I am my nephew's guardian.'

His eyes stayed steady on hers. '*Temporary* guardian.'

Charlie Law stared at the woman sitting opposite him.

His words were inflammatory. Intentionally so.

He knew he had no legal rights over Archie. Not yet anyway.

This was just a shot across the bows. He'd wanted to see how she reacted, and now he knew.

She looked not just stunned, but devastated.

Had he been a different man he might actually have felt sorry for her. But pity was not an emotion he indulged. With pity came weakness, and he didn't allow weakness in himself or tolerate it in others.

He stared at her steadily, ignoring the beat of desire pulsing through his blood.

His father was an enormously wealthy man who owned many fabulous works of art. A large number of them were paintings and sculptures of beautiful women.

But none of those women came close to Dora Thorn.

With pale skin the colour of ivory, tousled blonde hair and smudged grey eyes, she looked like a Botticelli *Venus*.

His jaw tightened. That was where the resemblance ended though.

He glanced down at the folder that Peter Muir had handed him. Beneath it, in a separate file, was a report compiled by his security team here in London. The contents of that report had been neither revelatory nor significant. They had simply served to confirm his suspicions.

Dora Thorn might be beautiful and desirable, but she was also flaky, undisciplined and without the means to raise his half-brother appropriately.

Great social life, though, he thought coldly. She flitted between several sets of friends, and London seemed to be populated with young men whose hearts she had broken.

Clearly, though, she thought she was worthy of

more than some calf-faced student. No doubt she thought she would find richer pickings among the gamblers at Blakely's.

Gritting his teeth, he let his eyes flicker over her beautiful face, then drop to the curve of her hips.

He could forgive her some things—that pencil skirt and blouse made her look as if she was dressing up in someone else's clothes—but blood was an indelible marker of character.

He had worked with her sister, talked to her, *trusted* her, and she had been a liar. Though no actual lies had been told, she had been living a lie…sneaking around with his father—his *married* father.

Dora might not look like her, but it was what lay beneath the skin that mattered more than shared features.

On paper, she spelt trouble.

In the flesh—

His brain froze on the word, and his eyes were drawn inexorably to the glimpse of pale skin where her grey silk blouse had parted. He gritted his teeth. She was trouble with a capital T, and then some.

Three nights ago he'd gone to the casino where she worked. He'd told himself that he was simply scoping out the opposition. London was a 'possible' on his list of locations for expanding the Lao empire, and Blakely's was a small, but profitable casino.

The truth, though, had been that he'd wanted to see her—to check out Dora Thorn in person.

Something hot and primal snaked over his skin.

He knew enough about casinos to know in advance that her uniform would have been carefully designed to convey modesty, while hinting at what lay beneath, and yet watching her walk across the room had been a shock.

As she'd leaned forward to decant drinks from her tray onto the table, he'd noticed a man at the bar glance over, his eyes narrowing appreciatively, and Charlie had felt a rush of anger. At him, a nameless stranger, at her, for being there, and most of all with himself, for feeling anything.

Emotions were a distraction—particularly in this instance. He was here in London for one day and with one purpose. To fulfil his father's dying wish. To bring his father's baby son back to Macau.

And it was going to happen. No matter that

he had this questionable hunger for a woman he didn't like or trust.

His father didn't countenance failure, and neither did he. He had made a promise, and not keeping that promise would mean bringing dishonour to himself, to his name, to his family.

'Let's keep this simple, Ms Thorn. And civil.' His eyes swept over her face. 'We *are* almost family, after all.'

'Civil?' She almost spat the word at him. 'You lured me here under false pretences. How is that civil?'

He shrugged. 'I assume you had your reasons for coming here.' Leaning forward, he pushed the folder Peter Muir had given him across the table. 'I think you will find everything in here that you want.'

Her grey eyes widened. 'I don't *want* anything from you.'

He watched two spots of colour spread over her cheeks, her face betraying the lie. His body hardened to stone. So she felt it too.

'My apologies,' he said calmly. 'I should have said "need" rather than want.'

He could almost see the war raging inside her. Her curiosity battling with her indignation.

Slowly he counted to ten and then flipped open the folder.

'You have a negative cashflow problem.' He flicked over a page. 'Put simply, your outgoings exceed your earnings and are likely to continue doing so.'

Her face jerked upwards. 'How do you know that?'

He watched her jaw tighten.

'Oh, I get it.' She shook her head, her eyes narrowing. 'Very classy. You know, you should probably change your name to Lawless. It would be more appropriate.'

'I don't know what you're talking about,' he said blandly, enjoying the flush of anger in her eyes. 'But I do know that if you carry on as you are it won't be long before your financial situation becomes an issue.'

He paused and let his eyes drift over her slowly. 'Archie's guardian needs to be capable of caring for him and providing for him. Hard to do that without money. And you are what would be classed as "low income with no prospects".'

The muscles in her face tensed.

'I'm sure the powers that be know that some things are more important than money,' she retorted. 'Not that I expect *you* to understand that.'

'Meaning?' he said softly.

She leaned forward, smiling coldly. 'Meaning that when your father was alive he had no interest in Archie, or even the concept of Archie. He wanted sex from Della—not a son.'

Charlie blinked, caught off guard by the bluntness of her words as much as the emotion in her voice.

'Your sister knew exactly what she was getting into. She knew he was married—'

'Yes, she did. But you don't know what Della was like.'

Wrong, he knew exactly what she had been like. She had been one in a long line of his father's mistresses, all of them hoping, believing, that Lao Dan would make her his wife.

His chest tightened and, changing the direction of his thoughts before they could cross into dangerous territory, he shook his head. 'None of that is relevant to this conversation. What matters here is Archie, and his well-being, and we both know that I can offer him the very best of everything. If you sign this document, I can make your financial problems go away.'

Her breath hitched in her throat. 'So you're offering me a bribe?'

'I prefer to think of it as compensation.'

Her eyes dropped to the folder and he felt his heart skip a beat. Was she really going to sign it? His stomach clenched. For some reason he didn't understand he felt more disappointed than triumphant.

'That's a lot of zeros for one little boy and my compliance.'

She lifted her chin, her gaze turned hard, and the air between them seemed to thicken.

'But you know what? I happen to think you can't put a price on the privilege of raising a child. And, frankly, I'd rather keep my pride than have your "compensation" polluting my life.'

She was staring at him as if he was something she wanted to scrape off her shoe.

He felt his muscles twitch. *Seriously? She was trying to take the moral high ground, here?*

'Very noble. Very profound,' he said softly. 'And yet how easily you forgot the "privilege" of raising Archie when you called that adoption agency.'

The colour left her face and the fire faded in her eyes. 'Th-that's confidential,' she stammered.

'That doesn't mean it's not relevant.'

Reaching across the table, he picked up the document and held it out, and after a few seconds she took it. His muscles tightened, and he was surprised at the second stab of disappointment. He hadn't expected her to capitulate so easily.

There was a beat of silence and then she raised her head slowly, her chin jutting forward.

'Actually, I'll tell you what's relevant.' She paused. 'No, make that *critical*. And that is that no child—particularly my nephew—should be raised by someone like you. Someone who not only has an armoury of dirty tricks at his disposal but is more than willing to use them.'

Standing up, she crumpled the document and dropped it on the table.

'Keep your money, Mr Law. You're going to need it for when we go to court.'

Stepping neatly past him, she walked across the room and out of the door before he had time to stand.

CHAPTER TWO

LEANING FORWARD, CHARLIE picked up the small ox bone tile from the table, his fingers tightening around the curved edges.

Back in Macau, he played mah-jong most days, but whenever he was away from home it was hard to find a good enough opponent. Sometimes he grabbed a quick game with one of his off-duty security detail, and sometimes he resorted to playing it on his phone.

Mostly, though, it was enough simply to lay out the tiles. But this morning it wasn't having the same calming effect as usual.

Gritting his teeth, he stood up and walked slowly towards the floor-to-ceiling windows that ran three sides of his penthouse duplex. His dark eyes tracked the progress of a barge along the Thames as inside his head he tried to make sense of his current unsettled mood.

As a rule, his life ran like clockwork. A very expensive and accurate clock.

He was an early riser. A session with his personal trainer started his day, followed by a shower and then breakfast. Occasionally he drove himself to work in his discreet black Bentley Mulsanne. But mostly a chauffeur-driven car was waiting to take him to the Golden Rod.

His father's huge casino hotel was the equivalent of Mayfair on the Monopoly board of Macau's Cotai Strip. As well as round-the-clock gaming, guests could shop, swim, work out or just enjoy Michelin-starred dining.

Its sister hotel, the Black Tiger, was a more recent development. Smaller, and set away from the over-the-top glamour of the strip, it was pitched at the high rollers—the serious players who didn't bother turning up unless the pot was worth a string of zeros.

The Black Tiger had been his own brainchild, and seeing it succeed was immensely satisfying. What mattered more was that its success had earned him the rarest prize of all—praise from his father.

Charlie worked hard seven days a week, dealing with all the behind-the-scenes details that kept a hotel and casino empire operating smoothly. But whatever happened during the day, he went back home for seven hours of un-interrupted sleep.

Yesterday had been different.

He had spent the day in meetings, and for per-haps the first time ever he had found it hard to focus. His mind had kept drifting from the task in hand back to that moment when Dora had stared at him, her eyes dark like storm clouds.

For some reason, those few half seconds had got under his skin.

She had got under his skin.

Her beauty. Her spirit.

And his failure.

Not to get her to take the money. That had never been anything more than bait—a way to get her attention, to get her good and mad so that she wasn't thinking clearly.

No, it had been his failure to stay detached that had made it impossible for him to concentrate.

His mouth tightened into a line of contempt.

It was the first time he could ever remember his libido overriding his logic and pragmatism.

Last night, with a discipline formed over many years, he had forced himself to fall asleep, but in the early hours he had woken in a panic, his sheets tangled around his body, his muscles straining against memories of those nights in his parents' house in Macau.

As a child, he had slept badly. 'Night terrors', his mother had called it, but the truth was that it had been the days he'd dreaded.

She was beautiful, his mother. Exquisite, his father had used to say, when he'd still been able to bear being in the same room as her.

His shoulders tensed.

Personally, he could think of better words to describe Nuria Rivero—'unhappy' being the most apt. Born into a Macanese family whose wealth was shrinking at a breakneck pace, she had felt the pressure to marry swiftly.

Marriage to his father had preserved her status, but as her power over her husband had diminished she had grown ever more frantic and fearful, and her son had borne the brunt of her fears.

His phone felt heavy in his pocket. He should call her—and he would. Just not right now. He wasn't in the mood.

He felt tense. His body was literally humming with energy—the kind of energy that he rarely felt these days, the sort that came from being thwarted.

Breathing out slowly, he rolled the tile across

his knuckles, reaching into himself, trying to find that familiar place of focus and calm.

The first rule of the casino was to leave your emotions at the door. It had been a condition of his joining his father's business that he learned to master his emotions, and it had taken him a long time but he had done so.

He breathed out slowly.

In comparison, it had taken only one brief meeting with Dora Thorn to rob him utterly of that hard-won ability.

Glancing down at the swift-moving water, he felt his pulse jump. His father used to say, 'Don't push the river. It will flow by itself.' But somehow he got the feeling that wasn't going to work with Dora. In fact, he'd lay money on it that, wherever she was right now, she would be building as many metaphorical dams as she could.

Dora Thorn.

When he'd first heard her name she had been nothing to him. He'd seen her as more of a nuisance than a serious obstacle in his path. But she was proving surprisingly tenacious—a regular thorn in his flesh, in fact.

The tile slipped from his fingers and, swearing softly, he reached down to pick it up. In the greyish light filtering through the window of the living room the tile looked almost luminous. His fingers twitched as he turned it over, remembering how she had looked at him at the lawyers' offices.

Dora's skin was exactly the same colour as the tile. He guessed it would be smooth and warm.

He breathed in sharply as he imagined peeling off her clothes, stripping her bare and splaying her out beneath him. Closing his eyes, the better to picture her, he felt his body harden.

Would that kissable pink mouth part in surrender?

Would her eyes flicker with the same fire as they had yesterday morning in the lawyers' office?

His eyes snapped open. Pocketing the tile, he leaned forward, resting his forehead against the cool glass, gazing down at the city beneath him.

He hadn't expected her to accept his offer.

But nor had he expected her to throw it in his face.

Actually, she had done more than throw it in his face—she had practically rolled up her sleeves and demanded they finish it outside.

His mouth twisted. Her challenge should have been easy to ignore. After all, it had been an empty threat. Like a featherweight stepping into the ring with a heavyweight, she might get in a couple of lucky punches but nothing that would cause serious harm.

And yet he couldn't help feeling a fleeting and unwilling twitch of admiration for her defiance.

He frowned as from across the room the intercom buzzed.

This apartment was one of several properties he owned in London. He liked its riverside location and the panoramic views across the city. Plus, the twenty-four-hour concierge team were unfailingly polite, efficient and engaged without being intrusive.

The intercom buzzed again.

Or they had been up until this moment.

Mouth hardening, he strode over to it, damping down his irritation. 'Yes?'

He heard the concierge give a nervous cough.

'I'm sorry to bother you, Mr Law, but there's someone here to see you—'

'Impossible,' he interrupted curtly. 'I made no such arrangement.'

'She says she's a family member.'

His hand hovered over the button. *She?* His mother and half-sisters were nearly six thousand miles away. So who, then?

He felt his jaw knot, the goading words he had spoken to Dora replaying inside his head.

'Let's keep this simple. And civil. We are almost family, after all.'

He nearly smiled. But instead he said quietly, 'Send Ms Thorn up.'

He stared across the apartment to the discreet lift doors. Twenty-four hours ago Dora had been itching to start a fight with him. But it would have taken no time and even less imagination for her to decide that it was a fight she didn't want.

Logically, her next option would be to flee—so from the moment she had stormed out of Capel Muir Fellowes his people had been keeping track of her. Or rather Archie.

But, truthfully, it had never crossed his mind that she would be doing the same to him, and he felt another unwilling flicker of admiration.

Like many people in his position, he took considerable care to leave the smallest possible digital footprint, even preferring to use shell companies to purchase properties overseas. It would have taken a considerable amount of effort to track him down.

He heard the lift arrive.

So she must want to see him badly.

A pulse of anticipation beat beneath his skin.

He'd always known that yesterday's meeting with Dora would not be the last. He had expected her to respond. That she had done so this quickly, and imaginatively, was just a bonus.

He watched the lift doors open.

Dora was sandwiched between two of his security guards. She looked ludicrously small, and her blonde hair was tied back in some kind of complicated braid that made her look younger than before.

Or maybe that was her lack of make-up. Not that she needed any.

But it was her clothing that made a muscle bunch in his jaw.

Gone was the figure-hugging pencil skirt and silky blouse and in their place were slouchy jeans, clompy black boots and a suede tasselled bag that looked as if it weighed more than she did.

The message was loud and clear, and it matched the defiant tilt of her chin. She'd come here to make a point.

Interesting, but ultimately pointless.

The house always won.

And she should know that better than anyone, given that she was working in a casino.

Dismissing the two men with a nod of his head, he held her gaze.

'Ms Thorn,' he said softly. 'Won't you join me?'

Eyeing him warily, Dora followed him through the apartment.

Wow, she thought silently, trying not to gape.

But it wasn't the beautiful understated interior that was making her breathe out of time.

In the twenty-four hours since she had last seen him, she had built up Charlie Law in her head to be a monster, skulking in the shadows. And yet here he was, clean-shaven, the tiger stripes in his dark hair gleaming in the pale sunlight that was creeping out from behind the grey clouds. He looked…not ordinary—he could never be that—but certainly not like the villain she had conjured up.

She glanced furtively up at him through lowered lashes. Just looking at him dried her mouth.

She had forgotten how innately imposing he was. He might not be wearing a suit today—or at least not a jacket—but he still had that air of power. So much so that his light blue shirt with its top button undone and loosened navy tie seemed only to emphasise his discipline and poise.

Her cheeks felt warm, and her pulse began to beat in her throat.

Unfortunately, the shirt also accentuated what lay beneath.

Her eyes fixed momentarily on the taut definition of muscle, and a flurry of awareness scampered over her skin. If someone had shown her a picture she would have assumed he'd been airbrushed. He was just too beautiful, too perfect to be real.

But he was real, and he was standing in front of her. With an effort she looked away, and gazed around the apartment.

Of course she already knew that the Lao family were fabulously wealthy. Della had sent her photos on her phone of Lao Dan's mansion in Macau, but it had been difficult to see much. This, though, was real.

Picturing Della's small terraced house, Dora felt a rush of panic. How was she supposed to compete with all this?

You don't have to, she told herself quickly. *You're Archie's guardian, and that isn't going to change if Charlie Law owns one penthouse or even a hundred.*

Dropping onto one of the huge leather sofas that barely filled a corner of the vast open-plan living area, he leaned back, resting one leg carelessly over the other. 'Would you like some coffee?'

She gave him a small, tight smile. 'No, thanks. I'd prefer to get down to business.'

He held her gaze, his eyes narrowing fractionally at hearing his own words in her mouth.

'So how did you find me? I hope it wasn't too expensive.'

Her heart pulsed high in her throat. It had taken quite a lot of phone calls, and a fair amount of emotional blackmail, but she had called in a favour with Pug, one of Della's old contacts.

She shrugged. 'Not everyone has to bribe and bully their way through life, Mr Law. Sometimes, if you ask nicely, people actually do what you want. You should try it some time.'

'Good to know,' he said softly. 'Next time I want anything from you, I'll ask nicely.'

The air thumped out of her lungs. She didn't know how to respond to that, and suddenly she had a fleeting but sharp memory of that moment when he had first looked into her eyes and she had felt that strange, unsettling wave of attraction.

Last night, when she had finally persuaded

Pug to tell her where Charlie Law was staying, she had expected to be given the name of a hotel. The idea that he had a *home* in the city where she and Archie lived had made her stomach turn into a ball of panic.

Clearly he didn't live here all the time, but as she'd sat last night, watching a documentary about tigers in Northeast China, she had realised that she didn't want to be like some poor, hapless deer.

This morning, standing outside, gazing up at his state-of-the-art penthouse, she still hadn't worked out what she was going to say to him. She'd just known that she wanted him to experience what it felt like being hunted and watched.

Being the prey, not the predator.

But now, in his apartment, she was starting to wonder if she had made the right decision in coming here. It wasn't just that she didn't know what to say. He seemed utterly unfazed by her presence.

'Why don't you sit down?'

She glared at him.

'Will I need to? Is trying to bribe me into handing over my nephew not big or bad enough for you? Have you got some other bombshell you want to drop on me?'

The tension in her body was making her voice sound high and breathless, but if he noticed he gave no sign of it.

'You brought the battle to *me*, Ms Thorn.'

She felt the fine hairs on the back of her neck rise.

Yesterday, his threats had been more subtle— just hints at the array of legal firepower and money he had at his disposal. But now he was being less coy. The gloves were off.

Her gaze darted involuntarily to his hand, resting negligently along on the armrest, and she remembered that sharp sting of heat as his fingers had touched hers.

In that moment, just for a few fleeting seconds, she had seen a different man beneath the smooth, controlled surface. A man without boundaries. A man willing to use those hands to stir and torment and pleasure his lover to the point of abandonment.

She felt her heart skip a beat, then speed up, and, feeling suddenly a little dizzy, she sat down.

'You're right. I did.'

The anger and audacity that had brought her here were rapidly dissolving. But she needed to say something. She couldn't just sit there and glare at him.

Sitting up straighter, she forced herself to meet his gaze. 'Look, I know your family is a big deal in Macau, and I'm sure you're used to throwing your weight around and getting your own way there. But we're not in Macau, and your name and your money don't mean anything here.'

She had half expected him to interrupt, to tell her that she was wrong, but he didn't say anything. Instead he just watched her impassively, letting silence fill the space between them until she thought she might scream simply to break it.

'In my experience, money is a universal language,' he said finally.

Her heart pounded fiercely. He was right. Rich people had that knack of getting what they wanted, but—

'Archie's not some business deal,' she snapped, her fluttering panic giving way to a punch of anger. 'And, excuse the pun, but I have the law on my side. Or at least the only law that matters.'

For a moment, he held her gaze, and then he shrugged dismissively. 'For now.'

'No, not just for now.' Her fingers tightened into fists, as his mouth flickered at one corner. 'I'm Archie's appointed guardian. If you want anything to do with him, you have to go through *me*.'

'But of course,' he said softly. 'Isn't that why you're here?'

She stared at him, her heart bumping against her ribs as he shifted in his seat, the movement making his shirt tighten distractingly against the contours of his chest.

'Or did you have some other more *personal* reason for coming today?'

Her eyes flew to his, a quiver of heat running down her spine, and she breathed out unsteadily, trying to ignore the way his words were making her pelvis clench.

He was playing with her. And the more fiercely controlled he became, the more she started to unravel. But what was she supposed to say? *I wanted to feel like a tiger, not a deer.* That would sound completely mad.

She took a steadying breath. 'When he was alive, your father didn't want anything to do with Archie.'

'But I'm not my father,' he replied quietly. 'And I *do* want to know Archie. Very much.' His gaze held hers steadily. 'Ms Thorn, I understand and respect your loyalty to your sister—but, like it or not, Archie is my father's son and my half-brother.'

She felt her stomach clench. Her pulse quickened. Coming here today was supposed to catch him off guard. So why did it feel as if a trap was closing around *her*?

He couldn't possibly have known that she would come here, but she couldn't shift the feeling that that was exactly what had happened.

And now she was here.

With him.

In his apartment.

She felt suddenly very stupid and very small.

'Getting someone pregnant only makes a man a father in the most literal sense,' she said, trying to control her voice. 'Della did everything for Archie—she got up for him in the night, she carried him and bathed him and sang to him.'

Her heart thudded heavily in her chest. She had once sung to Archie too.

There was a tense silence.

'And now she's gone,' he said finally.

Dora looked away, blinking back sudden hot tears, her shock at his response buffering the pain beneath her ribs. Never—or not that she could remember anyway—had she met anyone as cold as him.

But then she'd never met Lao Dan. He had clearly taught Charlie Law everything he knew about ruthlessly going after what he wanted.

Like father, like son, she thought with a surge of anger. Except that Archie—Della's Archie—was Lao Dan's son too, and Dora couldn't imagine him being so controlled and detached. He was such a sweet, loving little boy…

Blocking her mind to the hollowed-out feeling that always accompanied thoughts about her sister, Dora sat forward. 'But I know what she would have wanted for him.'

'As do I,' he said quietly. 'She would have wanted him to be with you. You're his family.' His eyes were looking directly into hers. 'But so am I. He has my blood…my DNA…'

He paused, and something in his dark eyes made her throat tighten.

'And together we share a birthright.'

A birthright. Did he mean some kind of inheritance?

She glanced over at him. He was seemingly watching the river, but she knew that it was a pretence.

Heat shivered over her skin.

There was something connecting them—something gossamer-fine and yet tenacious, so that it wouldn't matter even if her eyes were shut. She would know where he was.

She could feel him.

And he felt it too.

Heading off the unsettling implication of that thought, she replayed his words in her head, letting anger swamp her panic.

'Birthright?' She shook her head. 'You know, for a moment there I actually thought there was another side to you. But everything comes back to money with you, doesn't it?'

Her eyes narrowed on his profile.

'Well, you're wasting your time—and mine. Like I already told you, I don't want your money.'

'Maybe not.' Now he turned to look at her. 'But it's not your money to refuse, is it?' he said without preamble.

The simple question made her spine snap to attention and she glared at him. He was messing with her head, twisting her intentions.

'I know what you're doing,' she said shakily. 'But don't try and make me out to be the bad guy here. I'm not the one throwing around bribes and making oh-so-subtle threats.'

'No, but you are deliberately refusing to even discuss something that would give Archie a better life.'

He was lounging on the sofa with his legs sprawled out in front of him. Her pulse jumped. Take away the shirt and tie and he'd look almost like one of her mates, recovering from a very late night, she thought. But Charlie Law wasn't suffering from a hangover. Beneath his stillness she knew he was thinking, deliberating, choosing his next words with meticulous care.

'Do you really think that's what Della would have wanted, Dora?'

She blinked. It was the first time he'd called her by her name, and hearing it spoken in his soft, precise voice made her insides tighten.

'And how exactly do you think Archie will feel when he gets old enough to understand what you did? What you so freely rejected on his behalf. Do you think he'll see it the same way?'

She felt suddenly dizzy.

He might have called it compensation, but yesterday when he'd offered her money she had felt unequivocally righteous in refusing him, refusing what was essentially a bribe. But this felt different.

It *was* different.

This time he wasn't offering her money.

He wasn't offering *her* anything.

His dark eyes were level with hers, and she could see herself reflected there.

A knot formed in her stomach. How many times had she had to do this? Be forced to look at herself through someone else's eyes and find herself wanting.

Tabitha, her mother, had been the first—although, to be fair, her mother hadn't really stuck around long enough to dislike what she saw. Dora's father had made up for that, though. She shivered. David's blue eyes were so like Della's, but where her sister's had been full of love, his had always expressed a kind of disappointed boredom.

But this was not the moment to be thinking about her parents.

'Archie is my flesh and blood too,' she said stiffly. 'There's nothing I wouldn't do to give him the best possible life.'

He studied her face. 'Good. Then I'll call my housekeeper in Macau and let her know that you and Archie will be coming to stay. Shall we say for three weeks?'

Dora watched as he stood up and walked towards the window, pulling out his phone. She was mute—paralysed with shock and confusion. Inside her head, her heartbeat was booming like a cannon, and for a moment she thought she must have misheard him. But then she looked at his face, and she knew there was nothing wrong with her hearing.

'No.' She stood up, her whole body trembling with anger. 'We shall not say that. I am not going to Macau with you, and nor is Archie.'

He stared at her, then slowly pocketed the phone. 'You said there was nothing you wouldn't do.'

She shook her head. 'I didn't mean I'd take a trip to Macau.' She was losing track of the conversation. 'You said he has a "birthright"...'

'Everything comes back to money with you, doesn't it?' he said softly.

In that moment she hated him. Hated the way he could turn words on their head and inside out, and the way her made her feel one step behind.

The silence stretched out and curved across the room as he left the window and walked towards her.

She took an immediate defensive step back, felt her anger stalling, then panic and something else flaring hotly over her skin as he stopped in front of her.

'Archie's going to be one next week. What better time could there be to introduce him to his family than his birthday? And that's what I want, Dora. For Archie to come to Macau to meet his family. To see his home. To spend time with his half-brothers and -sisters. He has a right to do that. And I know it's what your sister wanted too.'

Their gazes locked.

'She wrote my father letters. He showed me some. Nothing private—just words about how much she loved Macau. What it meant to her. What family meant to her.'

Dora swallowed. It was true. Della had loved Macau. And she knew that more than anything her sister had dreamed of living there as a family, with Lao Dan and Archie.

But Della hadn't been the only one with dreams of family life. Their mother's absence and her father's indifference were like wounds that refused to heal. She knew what it felt like to be cast adrift, and she couldn't inflict a version of her life on Archie.

As if sensing her thoughts, Charlie took a step forward. 'Could you do that for her, Dora? Could you put aside your feelings, your doubts, your *life*, and bring Archie to his home in Macau? For Della?'

For a moment she struggled to find words. She was aware of nothing but the pounding of her heart and his eyes on hers—dark, steady, compelling. Her love for her sister felt like a weight. And there was guilt too. Remembering her phone call to the adoption agency, she felt sick with regret and shame.

She felt as if she was being pulled in opposite directions.

She knew Della would want her to go. And she knew Archie had an immutable right to know his father's family as well as his mother's.

But she was scared. Scared of losing *her* family.

Right now, she mattered to Archie—and she didn't want to stop mattering, like she had with everyone but Della.

And she was scared of this man. Of his sense of purpose, his implacability. Scared, too, of this confusing and unsettling connection between them.

But was it such a big ask? Surely she could do this? She could offer up a few weeks of her life in exchange for all those sacrifices her sister had so willingly made for her.

'Okay,' she said, not meeting his eyes. 'But I can only do two weeks at the most—and maybe not even that long.'

It was just something to say, really—a tiny spoke in the wheel of the juggernaut that was Charlie Law—but she needed him to know that he couldn't have everything his own way.

'We can finalise the details further down the line,' he said blandly.

She was no more reassured by the reasonableness of his manner than she had been by his relaxed dress code.

'I need to go now,' she said abruptly.

'Of course. Let me show you out.'

It wasn't necessary. Even in her distracted state she could have found her way to the lift. But he was already moving. Keen to make her escape, she swung round and began to follow him, but as she did so the fringing on her bag caught on something.

She stumbled, and would have fallen, but with lightning reflexes Charlie caught her, his hands sliding round her waist and holding her upright.

Her fingers curled into his biceps and for a second she stared at him wide-eyed, a prickling heat chasing her pulse round her body. He was so close she could see the starburst of black in the brown of his iris.

Too close.

All the air was punched out of her lungs. His skin was as flawless as his features, and his scent teased her senses. He smelled of rosewood and cardamom and clean sheets.

Oh, but she wanted to taste him…to run her tongue over that beautiful unsmiling mouth.

Her heart was beating so hard she thought her ribs might break. She could feel his gaze, and his warm breath, and then his mouth almost touched hers, and her lips parted, and she was leaning into him, letting the heat of his body envelop her.

The lift bell pinged loudly, scaring her so that she breathed in sharply. Instantly she felt his hands tense around her waist, and before the doors were even half-open he had released her and taken a step back.

His face was expressionless, but his eyes were dark and mocking. 'I don't think so,' he said softly. 'I may be my father's son, and your charms are unquestionable, if a little one-dimensional for my taste. But I'm not my father, so I'm afraid you'll have to ply your wares elsewhere.'

Ply her wares!

Dora stared at him, her skin shrinking with horror both at his words and at her own behaviour.

'Well, I'm not my sister—and your charms are not just questionable, they're non-existent.'

Hating him—hating him more than she'd ever hated anyone in her life—she sidestepped past him, and walked as fast as it was possible to walk without running into the lift.

His dark eyes trapped hers. 'I'll be in touch, Ms Thorn.'

Meeting his gaze, she felt her heart slam against her ribs. It was a promise, not a threat.

As the doors closed, she leaned back against the walls, shaking from head to toe.

It was bad enough that she had leaned in to kiss a man who despised her. What was infinitely worse was the fact that she'd agreed to spend two weeks under his roof in Macau.

CHAPTER THREE

IT WAS A GREY, rainy day when Dora and Archie left England. Arriving in Macau felt like waking in the middle of a Technicolor dream.

She'd had no real idea what to expect. All she'd really known was that Della had been in love with the place.

Her mouth twisted.

More accurately, her sister had been in love with Lao Dan—and to her Macau *was* Lao Dan.

She glanced out of the window at the vivid egg-yolk-yellow sun. According to the internet, Macau was 'a vibrant mash-up of old and new, East and West', and probably on closer inspection that would be true, she thought, stifling a yawn.

But her first impression was that she had never seen so many people—except maybe on Oxford Street at Christmas.

And they were all so busy.

Eating, and shopping, and doing Tai Chi in the

little parks between the roads—roads that were jammed full of every conceivable form of transport from rickshaws to Rolls-Royces.

Beside her, her so-called 'assistant', Li, leaned forward and pointed proudly at a large glossy black car as it cruised smoothly past them. 'See the crest on the door? That belongs to the Black Tiger—Mr Law's hotel casino,' she added as Dora stared at her blankly. 'VIP guests have exclusive use of the cars during their stay.' She smiled. 'They are very popular.'

Dora smiled back, but she felt her stomach flip over as she caught a glimpse of the crest—the head of a snarling black tiger.

No wonder he'd chosen that name for his casino, she thought. The tiger was a symbol of power and strength, and of course it was also stunningly beautiful.

Her heartbeat skipped.

But being beautiful didn't change a tiger's nature. No matter how soft its fur, it still had sharp fangs and claws. And Charlie Law might have used persuasion, not force, to get what he wanted, but beneath that civilised exterior lurked the heart of a predator, and she needed to remember that when she was dealing with him.

She felt her stomach perform another slow

somersault. She had been damping down a feeling of uneasiness since leaving Charlie Law's penthouse five days ago. Now, though—now that she was actually here in Macau—it was threatening to rise up and swamp her.

She'd been dreading the flight over ever since his incredibly efficient PA, Arnaldo, had got in touch with her and told her when a limousine would pick her and Archie up.

The idea of flying sixteen hours on a plane with an eleven-month-old baby had appalled her, but the prospect of flying with Charlie on one of the Lao family's private jets had been even more appalling.

Fortunately, he'd had to fly back to Macau early, so she'd been spared that ordeal. But it had only been a temporary reprieve, and now the clock was counting down to when she would have to face him again.

Her chest tightened as she remembered their last encounter in his apartment. Or, more specifically, those few tense, tantalising moments as they'd waited for the lift to arrive.

What would have happened if her bag hadn't got caught? Or if she hadn't tripped? Or he hadn't caught her?

Her cheeks felt hot.

Or, more worryingly, what would have happened if the lift hadn't arrived when it had?

She had been asking herself those same questions over and over again since it had happened.

Except *nothing* had happened, she told herself.

Her body tensed, and memories of what *hadn't happened* crowded her head.

He had been so close. Even now she could still feel how it had felt—the heat and the dizzying maleness of his body, the intensity of his dark eyes on hers. She had been mesmerised, rooted to the spot, drawn into his gaze so that the world had been reduced simply to the two of them, with her heartbeat drowning out everything else.

But it didn't matter that the fierce hunger inside her had been momentarily reflected in his face. From now on there were going to be no more 'what ifs'.

She glanced over to where her nephew sat in his car seat, ignoring the view outside the window and gazing in rapture at his octopus activity toy, his little hands clenching and unclenching with excitement at his reflection in a tiny rectangle of mirror.

This trip was for Archie's benefit.

And nothing—certainly not some insane attraction to a man she didn't like very much, and didn't trust—was going to jeopardise that.

As the limousine turned off the highway a sick feeling began to unravel in her stomach. Turning to Li, she said quickly, 'How far are we from Mr Law's house?'

'Around twenty minutes. It is a very beautiful area. Very secluded and private. Very secure. Perfect for children.'

Dora tried to smile. Secluded. Private. Secure. *Great. It sounded exactly like a prison.*

The sick feeling in her stomach was intensifying and, reaching over, she stroked Archie's face. Immediately he gazed up at her, his mouth curving into a smile that made her heart contract.

She felt a nibble of guilt. He'd hardly slept on the flight and he was tired. His eyes were practically popping out of his head, and his tiny baby brain probably thought it was lunchtime. But on Macau time she would be giving him his tea soon and getting him ready for bed.

She bit her lip, and not for the first time wondered if she'd made the right decision bringing Archie here.

All the experts said that babies needed certainty, and after everything that had already happened in his short life, wasn't that especially true for him?

She just needed to be more decisive, more definite.

Like Della.

Like Charlie.

She tensed, not wanting to throw even the smallest unspoken compliment in his direction, but she knew she was right.

If their positions were reversed, *he* wouldn't still be dithering over whether he was doing the right thing. He had the kind of focus and determination she had only ever found when she sang. Up on stage, in the circle of the spotlight, was the only place where she felt centred and whole.

Not any more, though.

Her chest tightened, as she remembered the clammy horror of *that* evening. It had been her first performance after Della's death. Nowhere fancy…just a club.

She shivered. She could feel it now: the heat of the spotlight, the sudden hush dropping like the curtain at the end of a performance.

Except it hadn't been the end.

Or maybe it had.

A man like Charlie would never understand how it felt to lose control like that. Whatever obstacles got in his way, he would find ways to get around them. Nothing and nobody would stop him from getting what he wanted.

Remembering how badly she had wanted to lean into him, she shivered. If he had wanted to lean into her she would have been in big trouble. Although why she was even thinking about that was a mystery, given that he couldn't have made it clearer that whatever he felt for her was against his better judgement.

'Are you cold, Ms Thorn?'

Dora looked up. Li was staring at her, her beautiful face creasing with anxiety. 'I will tell the driver to turn down the air-conditioning.'

'No, it's fine. Really. I'm not cold. Or warm,' she added quickly.

Charlie might think she was a world-class screw-up, but it was clear that his staff, and in particular Li, had been briefed to not just meet her needs but anticipate them with alarming speed.

The temperature in the limo suddenly ceased to matter as the car began to slow.

'We are here.' Li beamed as two towering security gates swung open. Five minutes later, the limo came to a smooth stop.

Given Charlie's foreboding manner, she'd been

half expecting a stone fortress. But, although his home sat behind high walls, and was guarded with electronic gates, the house in front of her was an elegant testament to his wealth and position.

With its pale green walls and cream-coloured shutters, it looked as if it was made of icing. If it hadn't been smothered with swathes of wisteria, she wouldn't have believed it was real.

Her heart dipped and she instinctively held Archie closer as Li gave a small bow. But the dark-haired man stepping into the sunlight wasn't Charlie.

'Ms Thorn, welcome. My name is Chen, and I oversee the running of the house.' He gave a small, swift bow too, and then, smiling, made a second, smaller bow. 'And this must be Archie.'

Archie buried his head against her shoulder, and Dora frowned apologetically. 'Sorry, he's just really tired.'

'Of course. Let me show you to your rooms.'

Dazedly, Dora followed him into the house. Lack of sleep and a surfeit of adrenaline was making her feel a little light-headed, so that she barely took in her surroundings. Just felt an awareness of space and cool opulence.

'These are your rooms.'

Smiling, Chen stepped back, and Dora felt her face slacken. Charlie's apartment in London had been impressive, but this...

She turned slowly on the spot, her heart reverberating against her ribs. It was an East meeting West fusion, the decor effortlessly blending traditional Chinese aesthetics with the stealth luxury that was only available to the truly rich—people who didn't need to shout about their wealth.

Polished dark mahogany furniture, oriental rugs and cherry-coloured silk blinds offset the white marble floor perfectly, and the chrome-framed mirrors and lacquered chests added an art deco vibe.

Archie's bedroom made a lump form in her throat. She knew Della would have adored the simple cream-painted cot, but it was the beautiful hand-painted mural of monkeys and romping pandas and tigers that made Dora rub her face against Archie's silken hair.

Seeing with her own eyes what Charlie could offer Archie made her feel horribly anxious, but it would be churlish not to acknowledge how lovely it was.

'It's beautiful,' she said quietly. 'Gently,' she added as Archie made a grab for a display of delicate blossoms. 'These are beautiful too. What are they? They smell divine.'

'Plum blossoms.' Chen smiled. 'Mr Law asked for them specifically.'

He had?

Gazing at the delicate pale pink flowers, she felt a pulse of joy, brief as a heartbeat, dart over her skin.

But before she had a chance to question her reaction, a thought occurred to her. 'Is Mr Law not here, then?'

Chen's expression shifted slightly. 'Mr Law sends his apologies. Unfortunately there was a problem at the casino.'

She felt her shoulders stiffen.

A problem? Seriously!

Her pulse was darting in angry little bursts.

This had been *his* idea. He had cajoled and manipulated her into coming here, and she and Archie had flown halfway across the world, and now he'd stood them up because of a problem at his casino.

With an effort, she hung on to her indignation. It wasn't Chen's fault that his boss was a scheming, selfish bastard, and she wasn't going to take it out on him. Working as a waitress at a casino had made her all too aware of how casually people exploited their positions of power.

'That's a shame.' She managed a smile as Archie yawned. 'Perhaps you could show me the kitchen? I think this little one needs to eat and then go to bed.'

As it turned out, she didn't need to go to the kitchen.

Before they'd left England, someone had called her requesting a list of Archie's favourite foods. And, although she'd rolled her eyes at the time, watching her nephew now, wolfing down his favourite meal of cheesy tomato pasta, prepared by the somewhat bemused chef, Jian, she had to admit that Charlie's obsessive need to be in control of everything had its plus points.

Not that she'd forgiven him for not being here earlier, she thought, as she tried to guide a wriggling Archie into his sleepsuit.

Even though he was shattered, she'd expected him to play up when she tried to put him in the cot. Since Della's death he'd grown clingy at bedtime, and she'd been letting him stay up later and later. But, incredibly, he went straight to sleep.

More incredibly still, she felt bereft.

She realised she'd grown used to cuddling up

with him in the evenings, and without him she suddenly felt close to tears, and homesick for their small, cosy living room.

Probably she was tired too, although, actually, she didn't feel tired at all. Maybe she just needed to eat something.

She took one last look at Archie, picked up the baby monitor and, leaving the bedroom door slightly ajar, crept out onto the landing, turning right towards the stairs.

Back in London, even at night, the streets were never silent. There was always a car alarm going off somewhere or the distant sound of police sirens. This house, in comparison, wasn't just quiet—there was a stillness to it that was both calming and unnerving.

Her pulse jumped.

It was a quality this home shared with its owner.

Her eyes flickered to the left. Those rooms hadn't been part of the guided tour.

Charlie's rooms?

Pulse accelerating, she took a hesitant step forward, curiosity fighting against common decency.

You can't, she told herself urgently. *You're his guest.*

But he won't know.

She bit her lip. Della would have been mortified.

But she won't know either.

Breathing out unsteadily, she glanced back into the silent house. It was incredibly rude to snoop. Her mouth twisted. Almost as rude as not turning up to welcome your guests. And it wasn't as if she was going to steal anything.

Besides, right now Charlie Law wasn't just a stranger, he was an enigma. It was only natural to want to find out more about this man who had dragged her halfway around the world.

Holding her breath, she opened the door, feeling a bit like Bluebeard's latest wife. But there was no terrifying chamber of secrets. On the contrary, his room was similar in style to her own, although it definitely had a more masculine feel.

Heart pounding, she ran her fingers lightly over the dark grey bedcover and breathed in, her nostrils flaring.

She could smell rosewood and cardamom. It was almost as if he was here.

Her skin tightened. With legs that felt wooden

she turned slowly. She felt her breathing waver, then stall in her throat.

Charlie was standing in the doorway, his dark eyes fixed on her face.

'See you anything you like?' he asked softly.

Charlie stared at Dora in silence. She was gaping at him as if she couldn't believe what she was seeing, and he understood completely how she felt.

He couldn't believe what he was seeing either.

It was tempting to think she was just a figment of his imagination. Except that in the feverish dreams that plagued his nights she wasn't wearing nearly as much clothing. Nor were her hands just stroking his bedding...

His body hardened, blood throbbing through him with punitive force. He gritted his teeth. His eyes weren't lying. Dora Thorn wasn't an illusion—she was here, in his room, her blonde hair loose around her face, her pink mouth parted in shock.

'I was just looking—'

'Why stop at looking?' He inclined his head towards the bed. 'Go on...get in. Make yourself comfortable.' Staring at her steadily, he paused, then said, 'But if this is some kind of clumsy attempt to lure me beneath the sheets, I'm afraid I'm going to have to disappoint you.'

'*What?*'

Her chin jerked up, cheeks reddening, eyes widening with shock and fury. 'I don't want to get into your bed—and I certainly don't want to get in it with *you*.'

She was lying. He could hear it in the urgency of her denial, see it in the pulse jumping at the base of her throat, and he felt his own pulse quicken in response.

'Yet here you are in my bedroom,' he said coolly.

'I told you. I was—'

'Looking?' He paused, holding her gaze. 'Is that what you call it in England? And there I was thinking you were snooping.'

She had the grace to look uncomfortable at that. He watched with some satisfaction as two flags of colour unfurled across her cheekbones.

'Fine. I was snooping,' she admitted. 'Happy now?' She glared at him. 'I was just curious.'

'About…?' he prompted.

She looked up at him; her cheeks were still pink, but her eyes met his.

'About you, of course. You're Archie's half-brother. I was trying to work you out.'

'And you thought looking at my bedlinen would shed some light on that?' He raised an eyebrow. 'Would you like to take a look at my bathroom too? Perhaps my choice of toothpaste might be illuminating.'

Her eyes—those glorious grey eyes—flashed with indignation like a tropical storm rolling in from the South China Sea.

'You are such a hypocrite. You had no qualms whatsoever about poking around in *my* life. Oh, sorry,' she said, without a hint of apology. 'It wasn't you in person, was it? Well, just because you paid someone else to do it, doesn't give you the right to be all holier than thou.'

He stared at her, his muscles tightening beneath his skin.

Was she really trying to equate the two things?

'If you want to know something about me, you could just ask,' he said softly. 'I have nothing to hide.'

Her mouth twisted. 'Only because you've probably got teams of people following you around, making sure your secrets are safe.'

He studied her face in silence. She was way off the mark. Nobody knew his secrets. How could they? Sharing a secret required trust, and he didn't trust anyone. Didn't know how to trust.

As Lao Dan's son he was privileged and pampered. He'd grown up surrounded by opulence and excess. Nothing was too expensive or too rare. His father had taught him that everything had a price.

Particularly trust.

His father's trust had had to be earned, and re-earned, again and again. He'd had expectations, and any failure to meet those expectations had had consequences. Failure had not been tolerated, and in some cases not forgiven.

As a child, it had been a hard lesson to learn, but it had taught him early on to rely on no one but himself, and that self-reliance and discipline had ended up being more useful than the three years he'd spent at business school.

'I have no secrets, Ms Thorn,' he said calmly. 'And no soul either.'

Her eyes snapped to his, flaring with fury, and for the space of a heartbeat he wanted to take that fire and turn it into a different kind of heat, make her body quiver as it had done when she'd stumbled into his arms.

'Sixteen hours,' she said slowly. 'Sixteen hours on a plane and another two hours in a car. That's how long it took us to get here. And we came all that way because *you*—' she jabbed her finger at his chest '—told me you wanted to spend time with Archie. Only you haven't so much as asked where or how he is. What kind of man does that? Drags a baby to the other side of the world and then doesn't even bother to see him.'

There was a faint shake to her voice.

'But then why should I be surprised? You've probably been raised from birth to think you're better than everyone else. Well, you're not. You're just a selfish, spoilt—'

'If you'd just let me—' he began, but she shook her head violently.

'Oh, please, spare me your explanations.'

Her face was pale and set, and he could hear that she was still angry. But beneath the anger there was a note in her voice, a mix of fear and defiance, that pulled at something inside him.

'Dora.'

He took a step closer, moving without thinking, and she breathed in sharply, recoiling away from him as if he was a cobra.

'Don't touch me.'

He didn't know if it was the hoarse panic in her voice or the fact that he'd let down his guard and almost allowed himself to feel sorry for her, but suddenly he'd had enough of this petulant, self-righteous child acting as if he was some monster from the mountains.

'I wouldn't dream of it,' he said, with deliberate calm. 'It's been a long day and I am tired and hungry. So, if you don't mind, I'm going to go and get something to eat.' He glanced pointedly around the room. 'Feel free to continue "looking". But remember—no touching.'

Her eyes narrowed.

'I wouldn't dream of it,' she snapped. 'Now, if *you* don't mind, I'm going to go and check on Archie. He's your brother, in case you've forgotten.'

She turned and flounced out of the room.

Gritting his teeth, he yanked off his tie and tossed it on the bed. He didn't ever lose his cool. But Dora Thorn pressed all his buttons. Made him see fifty shades of red. He felt like shaking her.

Loosening the top button of his shirt, he made his way downstairs, trying to reinstate the legendary self-control that had gained him a reputation for being ice-cold in and beyond his casinos.

The kitchen was cool and quiet. He preferred not to eat heavily in the evening, and if he wasn't dining at the hotel Jian prepared him a light supper in advance. But, delicious as it looked, he was too wound up to eat.

His spine stiffened. A week ago this had seemed so straightforward. Legally, he knew it would be a challenge to overturn her temporary guardianship, and almost on a whim he'd devised a less conventional strategy: bring her to Macau and persuade her to see the benefits for Archie of a life with him.

But now it was in play he was beginning to wonder if perhaps challenging her guardianship would have been easier. It would certainly have been better for his blood pressure and his temper.

Remembering the way her grey eyes had snapped with fury as she'd accused him of being selfish and spoilt, he felt the muscles of his arms bunch against his shirt. He might have had every material comfort, but he'd had to earn his place in the Lao family.

Dora had no idea. She was impossible. Irrational. Utterly unreasonable.

How was he even in the wrong anyway? *She* had been snooping in *his* room.

His mouth twisted a fraction. That was twice in under a week she had invaded his personal space.

Glancing up, he felt his whole body tense. *Make that three times.*

Dora was standing in the doorway—though 'hovering' might be a better description.

He shook his head slowly. 'I really don't think—'

'I'm sorry.'

Leaning back against the counter, he stared at her in silence. Whatever he'd been expecting her to say, it hadn't been that.

'I don't think I heard you correctly.'

'I'm sorry.' She inched forward, her grey eyes watching him warily. 'I shouldn't have gone into your room. It was wrong. But I did it because I was angry.'

She was speaking fast, her words almost running into one another.

'I was angry with you. I thought you'd be here to meet Archie. And then you weren't. I know he's little, and he doesn't understand, but you didn't even ask about him…'

Her face was taut. In fact her whole body was taut—as if she was holding herself in. His shoulders tensed. She wasn't as good at it as he was. But then she probably hadn't had as much practice.

'I saw the monkey,' she said quietly. 'Why didn't you tell me that you'd gone to see Archie?'

He hadn't wanted to turn on the light, so it had

been difficult to make out the little boy in the darkness, but he'd placed the cuddly monkey at the end of his cot.

'I tried.' His tone was harsh and, watching her bite her lip, he thought that maybe it was too harsh. 'But not hard enough. Look, Dora, I wanted to be here to meet Archie—only somebody lost their child at the hotel. I couldn't just leave. It was fine—he was fine,' he added, catching sight of her expression. 'He was hiding under a table. But the parents were very distressed and it took a long time to calm them down.'

He glanced down at his untouched meal.

'Are you hungry?'

In answer her stomach gave a loud, complaining rumble.

'Here.' He pushed the plate across the table towards her.

She tucked a strand of hair behind her ear and slid onto one of the seats. 'Thank you.'

He watched her sit down. Her cheeks were flushed and her pupils were dilated—both signs of being agitated.

Or aroused.

His breath caught in his throat and, needing to do something to force his mind away from his body's instant hard response to that distracting possibility, he said, 'Would you like something to drink? There's wine, or beer…'

Something shifted in her face.

'No, thank you.' She glanced away across the kitchen. 'You have a beautiful home. Is this where you grew up?'

'No.'

Her eyes rested on his face. 'But you did grow up in Macau?'

'Yes.'

'So do the rest of your family live nearby?'

They did. But their geographical proximity was not in any way reflected by familial closeness. His relationship with his half-sisters had always been fraught. How could it not be when they were all still fighting one another for their father's approval? Even after his death.

Charlie looked over at Dora, his skin tightening. He didn't want to think about that now, much less talk about it—and especially not with a woman who seemed to have this uncanny power to throw him off-balance.

'Some do,' he said.

She looked at him, her expression intent, curious. 'You don't like answering questions, do you?'

There was a beat of silence, and then, realising what she had just said, she smiled—a smile of such genuine sweetness that for a few half-seconds he forgot that he had found her snooping in his room. Forgot too, that she was the sister of his father's mistress.

All he could think about was how to make her smile at him like that all the time.

'Only if there's a purpose to them,' he said slowly.

'Oh, I have a purpose.'

She leaned forward. The soft glow from the downlights caught her face as she spoke, and he felt a sudden urge to run his finger over the curve of her cheekbone. To lean into her as she had leaned into him in his apartment.

A pulse twitched in his groin. The kitchen was large, and yet it felt suddenly disconcertingly intimate.

'You do?' he asked.

She nodded. 'I want to make Archie a family tree for his bedroom, so that after we go home I can show him all his family in Macau.'

His chest tightened, and he felt the disconnect between her words and his agenda opening up beneath his feet like a sinkhole.

How could he be so stupid? Was that all it took

to derail him? One smile and the memory of an almost-kiss?

Dora Thorn was beautiful and sexy, but he wasn't about to lose his head over a soft pink mouth. She wasn't here so they could finish what they hadn't started in London.

And if he was starting to forget that, then maybe now was the time to encourage her to keep her distance—*and* remind himself of the kind of woman she was.

'That's a lovely idea.' He paused. 'And to think if you'd gone through with the adoption you would never have been able to do that for him.'

There was a moment's silence, and then she inched backwards silently, sliding off the seat and tilting her head up so that her grey eyes were steady on his face.

'It must be nice to be so perfect. To live your life without ever making a mistake.' She put down her chopsticks carefully. 'I told you that I came here for Archie's sake, and I did. But I had an ulterior motive. I wanted to find out who you were. You see, I thought you couldn't possibly be as cold-blooded and manipulative as you appeared.'

Her lip curled.

'Guess I was wrong. Goodnight, Mr Law.'

CHAPTER FOUR

DORA HATED WAKING UP, and it was taking even longer than usual to drag herself out of the cocooning, comforting fog of sleep.

With an effort she rolled over onto her side and forced her eyes open.

For a moment she was utterly disorientated.

She had been dreaming about Della, and that holiday they had taken in Greece to celebrate her job in Macau. Instead of their usual modest apartment Della had splashed out and, as she glanced around at the unfamiliar luxury of her surroundings, Dora's first thought was that she was back in that hotel room.

And then she remembered.

Her heart lurched.

She wasn't in Greece with her beloved sister. She was in Macau with a man who thought she was a waste of space. A man who thought so little of her that he never missed an opportunity to remind her of that fact—as last night had proved.

Pushing back the covers, she rolled out of bed and headed to the bathroom.

But why should she care what Charlie Law thought of her? It didn't seem likely that she was going to see much of him anyway. He might have come up with a reasonable explanation for his no-show yesterday, but men in his position always put work before everything else—including their children and wives.

Except Charlie didn't have a wife.

She knew that because—and it was embarrassing to admit it—she had looked him up on the internet late one night.

And why shouldn't she have? she thought defensively. She was going to be staying in his house. And it wasn't as if she had gone through his bins or hacked his phone records. It was all there on the internet, for anyone to see.

Her insides tightened. Not that she cared one way or another if he was married. She would happily serve him up on a platter to any and all comers. He might look divine, but he was ruthless and single-minded and utterly devoid of any kind of empathy.

Remembering that crack he'd made about the family tree, she scowled.

Honestly, it was hard to imagine that he and Archie were actually related. Archie was so sweet and soft. Surely there was no way he would grow up to be like his horrible big brother.

And what gave Charlie Law the right to be so horrible anyway?

He had a charmed life. Fortune had blessed him with beauty, intelligence and wealth, with this incredible house, and with a father who had clearly thought so highly of him that he'd made him his successor to head the family empire.

Frankly, she'd swap his life any day for the hand *she'd* been dealt.

Her mother had found her so unnecessary she had walked out just months after she was born. And, although her father had stuck around longer, he'd never bothered hiding his indifference to her.

No one other than Della had ever shown her any love or support. And now she had lost the one person who had loved her no matter what.

Her chest tightened with a spasm of old pain and new anger. Picking up her toothbrush, she began brushing her teeth savagely.

If she could just go back in time—back to before she had gone downstairs and apologised to him.

Apologised!

She spat into the sink, her shoulders tensing. She had gone to check on Archie and found that toy monkey in his cot. Realising that she had accused Charlie of something he hadn't done, she had felt guilty.

Guilty.

Breathing out shakily, she spat that word into the sink too, along with a mouthful of toothpaste, and stalked back into the bedroom.

She had actually thought she'd misjudged him. Seeing the monkey, she had thought that there was a different side to Charlie, a hidden, *soft-hearted* side.

What a joke, she thought, glancing at her phone to check the time. If he even had a heart, which she doubted, it was probably made of stone, or—

Her thoughts screeched to an emergency stop. It was nine-thirty. Surely Archie would be awake by now. So why wasn't he babbling to himself or calling out to her?

With panic humming in her veins, she moved swiftly to the door adjoining their rooms.

Oh, no, no, no, no...

His cot was empty. Before the information from her eyes had even reached her brain she was out through the door and running down the stairs into the kitchen.

Pain was filling her chest. She was so stupid and gullible, bringing Archie here. Had she really believed that Charlie would only want him for a visit? That he wouldn't take this opportunity to—

'Ms Thorn...'

Cannoning into Chen, she gripped his arms.

'Where is he? Where's Archie?'

But before he could answer she heard Charlie speaking to someone outside, and she moved urgently towards the sound of his voice like a gundog following the scent of a rabbit.

For a moment she was blinded by the light, and then, as her eyes began to adjust, she felt her stomach start to churn with relief and anger.

Clutching his monkey, Archie was sitting in the sunshine. To be more exact, he was sitting on Charlie's lap, his dark eyes fixed intently on his half-brother's face.

She felt something scrape over her skin.

It was the first time she had seen the two of them together and, gazing at their identical dark heads, she felt her limbs go light.

Even before his birth she'd known Archie had half-siblings from Lao Dan's other relationships. But when Della had been alive it hadn't seemed to matter that much. They'd seemed more like characters in a film or a play than actual living people, so coming face to face with Charlie in London had been like watching an actor step through the television screen and into her living room.

Now, though, she could see that moment had been just a foreshock—a tiny seismic ripple across the landscape of her world.

The brothers turned towards her. Her breath caught in her throat as the ground lurched beneath her bare feet.

That first time in London, at the lawyers' offices, before she had even discovered they were half-brothers, Charlie had seemed familiar. But now, side by side, the resemblance between them was not just pronounced—it was astonishing. Their features were identical. Archie's were just smaller and still with some baby softness.

'Do-Do.'

Archie had spotted her, and she couldn't help feeling a childish twinge of satisfaction as his beautiful dark eyes widened and he reached out to her.

Refusing to meet Charlie's eyes, she lifted him up, hugging him close to bury her face in his silken dark hair. He was so precious to her, so important, and she loved him so much that even though she wanted to rage at Charlie for scaring her she knew she was incapable of speaking in complete sentences just yet.

Her eyelashes fluttered as she breathed in, Archie's baby smell calming the tremble in her body, and then, tucking him under her chin, she glared at Charlie.

'I didn't know where he was,' she said stiffly.

He stared at her steadily. 'He was with me.'

'But I didn't know that.'

Remembering the empty cot, she pressed Archie closer. Her skin was clammy and she could still taste the panic in her mouth, the real and potent fear that Charlie had spirited him away.

'You can't just take him without telling me.'

He shrugged, his handsome face expressionless. 'You were sleeping. I didn't want to wake you.'

Her eyes narrowed. She was only just about managing to hold on to her temper. 'Oh, please... are you really expecting me to believe you were being considerate? After what you said last night?' She didn't bother hiding her incredulity.

His eyes didn't leave her face. 'He was starting to get upset.'

'And I'm sure being picked up by some random *stranger* made him feel a whole lot better.' She made sure to put emphasis on the word 'stranger', and was suitably gratified when a muscle flickered in Charlie's cheek.

'But I'm not a stranger, am I, Dora?' He held her gaze. 'I'm his brother. And I'm sure I don't need to tell you how powerful the bond is between siblings—even those who have never met before.'

She wanted to hit him. Why did he have to look so together, so relaxed? Sitting there all smug and righteous, wearing an unobtrusive but no doubt paralysingly expensive espresso-coloured T-shirt and casual black trousers.

'You should have woken me up.'

'Perhaps you should have set an alarm.'

Excuse me? Her breath caught in her chest. Her pulse was jumping erratically, like a frog leaping between lily pads. Was he seriously trying to make this her fault?

Lifting her chin, she fixed him with the withering look that had silenced hecklers in clubs across London. 'Perhaps *you* shouldn't have dragged us both over here and then I wouldn't have been so tired.'

Annoyingly, his expression remained unchanged. Perhaps her powers of withering had been affected by jet lag.

'You're quite welcome to leave,' he said softly. 'Please feel free.' His dark eyes seemed to pierce hers. 'As long as Archie stays, of course. Your call.'

As long as Archie stays.

She was so strung up it took a couple of seconds for his words to hit home, and then slowly she felt a chill of understanding creep over her skin.

So that was what this was about.

Fury surged through her and she felt her whole body tense.

What a snake!

All that rubbish about not wanting to wake her up. Acting as if he cared. He didn't care about anything but getting his own way. Making her panic like that had been a way to knock her off-balance, make her look and feel out of her depth.

As if she needed any help doing either.

She felt her throat tighten. After their showdown at Capel Muir Fellowes she had been petrified he was going to escalate things. But then, at his apartment, he had backed down, offering this trip as a compromise. And, believing that he had accepted her as Archie's guardian, she had relaxed.

Only now she was here in Macau he was acting as though she was little more than an inconvenience. An annoyance. A nuisance to be sent packing at the earliest opportunity.

Thanks to her parents, it was a feeling she knew well. Not that they had ever cared about her feelings. Or her needs. It had always been what *they* felt, what *they* needed that mattered.

Her fingers tensed around Archie. It must be her—something she did—because now Charlie was following the same playbook.

But he could take a running jump if he thought she was going anywhere without Archie.

'Over my dead body,' she breathed. 'Or, better still, yours.'

He stared at her for a long moment, and then frowned. 'You're being serious?' His dark eyes mocked her. 'Sorry, it's just hard to feel that threatened by a woman in pink-and-white-striped pyjamas.'

Her heart thudded inside her chest. In her haste to find Archie she had not bothered to get dressed. But whose fault was that? she thought furiously.

Their eyes met, and then he tipped his head back a fraction, his gaze dropping from her face to her bare legs, lingering pointedly on the hem of her shorts where they hugged the curve of her bottom.

She felt her pulse stab at her throat as a flush of heat rose up over her shoulders. Against her will, she felt her blood rush. It wasn't fair for him to look the way he did and make her feel this way. Not when he was so contemptible.

'Thanks to you, I didn't have a chance to get dressed before I came downstairs,' she snapped. She softened her voice and expression as she turned to look down at Archie. 'But we like to stay in our jammies anyway—don't we, Buttons?' Shifting the baby onto her hip, she blew onto his neck, making him squirm. 'And we are on holiday after all.'

Charlie smiled then—the kind of smile a crocodile might give shortly before its jaws snapped shut on some poor unsuspecting prey.

'Me too.'

Her eyes jerked to his body, then moved to his feet.

Loafers. No socks.

She swallowed against the lump of apprehension building in her throat. He must be joking. Except Charlie didn't look like the kind of guy who would strut into work wearing loafers without socks. And one brief look at his face told her that he was being serious.

Her limbs felt suddenly stiff and wooden. She had selfishly been hoping he would be absent at work for most of the day—actually, for most of their stay.

'How nice,' she said in a small voice, ignoring the faint flicker of amusement in his eyes.

But what else was there to say?

She could hardly tell him she wanted him to go to work—not when she'd made such a song and dance about him not being there to welcome Archie. And, anyway, deep down it was why she had come all this way, wasn't it? So that he and Archie could spend some time together.

But she didn't have to stand here and watch him gloat about it.

'I'm going to take Archie to get dressed,' she said abruptly.

'He hasn't finished eating.' Charlie's eyes met hers. 'Why don't you stay? Have some breakfast?' He gestured towards the house. 'Jian will prepare anything you want.'

'I'm really not—'

'Please, Dora.' His voice softened too. 'Could we just call a truce? Just while you eat? Or, if you're really not hungry, just until you've drunk your coffee.'

Charlie gazed up at Dora, forcing his pulse to stay steady. He wondered if she had any idea how easy it was to read her thoughts. He could see the anger and resentment in her grey eyes. And the dark streaks of desire, like contrails in the sky.

A desire that mirrored his own.

He could feel it pulsing inside him, hot and urgent, crowding out all logic and sense.

His gaze snagged on her soft pink mouth and with an effort he kept it there. To let it drop to the smooth, enticing curve of her bottom would push his self-control to the edge of its limits.

She was maddeningly stubborn. Irrational and impetuous. In short, everything he avoided in a woman. And yet for reasons he couldn't fathom, he wanted her with an almost unbearable hunger.

Really, Charlie, you can't think of one reason?

Gritting his teeth, he moved his gaze, taking in her flushed cheeks and wary grey gaze. Yes, she was sexy and beautiful, and she was wearing miniscule pyjamas that showcased her mouthwatering body. But he had seen plenty of women in more provocative nightwear—beautiful, desirable women with soft mouths and smooth bodies. Women who didn't look as if they wanted to throw a suitcase at his head.

'Look, Dora. I know this is hard for you. It's hard for me too. But there has to be a compromise. We can't keep fighting or avoiding one another. Not if we're going to make this work for Archie.'

She stared at him, and again he could almost see the pros and cons ping-ponging back and forth inside her head.

'What's the catch?' she asked.

'Why would you think there is one?'

'Oh, I don't know, Charlie. Why would I?' She shifted the baby to her other hip. He was getting restless now.

'There is no catch. This is your first day in Macau. Archie's first day in Macau. I would rather, for his sake, that his two closest family members weren't at war with one another.'

He waited, reluctant to push. Whatever else Dora might be, she was no coward. Cornering her only made her come out fighting. He thought back to their first encounter at Capel Muir

Fellowes. Money clearly had no pulling power either.

Sensing that she was sifting through his words, trying to work out his agenda, he watched her in silence. When he had first learned of Della's death he had briefly considered challenging her sister's guardianship through the courts. The evidence against Dora was all there in black and white—*and red*, if you were talking about her bank balance.

But, even though he had access to some of the best legal brains in the world, he had quickly decided against it. There was a risk that it would get ugly. Worse, that it might become public—and he couldn't take that chance.

Family unity meant strength; any division or dispute risked making the Lao family look weak, and his father had taught him that *miànzi*—face—was everything.

Inadvertently, it had been Dora who had offered a solution. Her turning up at his apartment had suggested a more unconventional approach and, forgetting his usual need for obsessive preparation, he had invited her to Macau.

He didn't regret his uncharacteristic impulsiveness. His father had instructed him to do whatever was necessary, and here he had privacy and power.

His gaze drifted back to her face. But he had allowed himself to get distracted, and that was unconscionable given what was at stake.

Last night, after that 'incident' in the kitchen, he had decided it was time to rethink his strategy.

Dora was going nowhere—certainly not for these two weeks, anyway, and probably not in the years to come. Her accepting that would mean he could move towards his goal of formalising the length and frequency of Archie's visits.

Happily, he knew the perfect way to help make a case for that happening. Giving Dora a tour of the casino and hotel complex would show her exactly what kind of life he could offer his half-brother. Plus, it would set a much-needed businesslike tone for their interaction.

First, though, he needed her to sit down.

'There is no catch, Dora. I'm just offering you breakfast,' he said softly. 'And a chance for us to start again.' He smiled. 'I promise you can go back to hating me afterwards.'

That was the problem, Dora thought. She didn't hate him. Or rather her body didn't hate him.

But, whether she hated him or not, Charlie was never going to stop being Archie's half-brother, and they couldn't keep fighting for ever. Plus, it was difficult to resist some small softening in the stand-off between them.

Her pulse skipped a beat.

What would Della have done?

Her sister had always been so measured, so unselfish. She'd called it being the bigger person.

Perhaps this was the right time for her to be that person.

And perhaps Charlie had meant what he'd said, she thought ten minutes later.

The conversation was not what you might call 'flowing', but he was trying, and there were other compensations. The food was absolutely delicious, and for the first time since Della's death Dora's appetite had come back and she actually felt like eating.

A flutter of hope stirred inside her chest. Maybe other things might get back on track too. Not her career—that night in the club when she'd frozen on stage had put her off ever performing again. But it would be lovely to be able to sing for herself, for Archie…

'Oh, okay, then—but don't snatch.'

Archie was making a grab for her chopsticks

and, grateful for the distraction, she let him have them. Mostly he ended up dropping everything she gave him, but it wasn't worth an argument.

She knew she should be firmer with him, but it was hard. His tantrums didn't just scare her, they scared him. And when he was scared he wanted his mother, and she hated that. Hated watching his face crumple when Della didn't appear and, even though she knew it wasn't personal, she hated it when he pushed her away.

A shiver ran down her back. The idea that one day he might do it for real, like everyone else in her life she'd loved, was almost unbearable.

'He's far too young to use them.'

Charlie's voice broke into her thoughts and she glanced over at him warily. He was watching her, studying her, and instantly, predictably, she felt her face grow warm.

'I know that,' she said defensively. 'But it doesn't stop him wanting them.'

She was intently aware, not just of his gaze, but of him. His body. His breathing. It was crazy, but without even having to look she knew the tilt of his jaw, could sense the position of each of his limbs.

He leaned back. 'Some children get the hang

of it earlier, but right now Archie doesn't have the necessary coordination.'

She rolled her eyes. 'I suppose you learned this from your parallel life as a nursery nurse?'

There was a slight pause, and then he shook his head. 'No, just from having been a two-year-old who used to get immensely frustrated at not being able to feed himself.'

Their eyes met across the table and she felt her heart lurch. She didn't want to picture a two-year-old Charlie. It made him seem more human, and that was dangerous. And yet she couldn't resist this tiny glimpse into his life.

Or the chance to tease him.

'I'm surprised you can remember that far back.' Lifting her chin, she gave him a small, provocative smile. 'You know memory peaks in your early thirties and then starts to decline, so you're in the danger zone already?'

'Is that right?'

She felt his gaze curl around her body.

'I suppose you learned that from your parallel life as a neuroscientist,' he said softly.

Her pulse twitched. The intense focus of his gaze was making her skin sting. Nobody had looked at her in that way—not ever. Not even when she'd been doing auditions. It was almost as if he could see beneath her skin. It made her feel as if she was naked.

She glanced up at him, her breathing stalling. What would *he* look like naked?

The answering mental slideshow to that question made her feel light-headed and, quickly blanking her mind, she shrugged with forced casualness. 'Actually, I read it in a magazine on the flight over.'

He held her gaze. 'And do you read a lot of magazines?'

'No, not really. I prefer social media. I used to post a lot when—' She stopped herself. She was not going to go there with this uber-poised man, who probably had 'winner' stamped through him like a stick of rock.

'It's instant, more direct. But I'm guessing you're a bit more OG.'

'A bit more OG?' To her surprise, he laughed. 'That's not something I've been called before—but, yes, I suppose I am. I like to do things properly.'

Was that a dig at her? Dora stared at him, her spine tensing, suddenly alert. 'Well, luckily for you, you're in a position to make that happen.'

Taking a breath, she steadied her nerves and

smiled stiffly at Chen as he moved forward to clear her plate away.

'It's not so easy for other people.'

He nodded. 'I know. And I know that it must have been hard for you. Taking Archie on. Holding down a job. Dealing with all the paperwork.'

A knot was forming in her stomach. 'I manage.'

'You do,' he agreed. 'But you don't need to just "manage" any more. I can help. I *want* to help—if you'll let me.'

She felt nervous, like a mouse finding cheese in a trap; tempted but unconvinced. 'I suppose that would depend on what you mean by "help".'

His eyes were steady on her face. 'I thought you might welcome a bit of practical support. So I've arranged for someone to come in—a nanny. Her name is—'

'Thanks, but I'm good.' She spoke over him, her heart beating heavily in her chest.

'Shengyi is Chen's niece. Like him, she grew up on the mainland. She's well-qualified and experienced.'

Dora forced her features to remain impassive, but misery was clogging her throat. 'You mean in comparison to me?'

Sighing, he shook his head. 'This is not a criticism of you, Dora.'

'Liar.'

Somewhere behind her she felt Chen tense. But she had done this too many times in her life to care. Given people a second, a third, an infinite number of chances, only to realise that nothing had changed.

Someone was always ahead of her, or above her.

'I'm not lying, Dora.' His face had closed over.

'Of course not. And offering me money to give up Archie wasn't a bribe, I suppose?'

From nowhere, she felt tears blur her eyes. And suddenly she couldn't do it any more—couldn't stand there and have yet another person, particularly this man, point out her shortcomings.

Pushing herself to her feet, she shook her head. 'You know what is really sad? I think you actually believe that. You're so deluded by your power you either don't know or don't care what's true and what isn't. As long as you get what you want, you'll do or say anything.'

His eyes narrowed. 'I would prefer it if you didn't speak to me like that in my home, in front of my staff.'

'Well, I'd prefer it if you didn't speak to me at all.'

She flung the words at him, wishing they were the beautiful, intricately patterned porcelain cups and saucers on the table. Instantly, she regretted it.

Maybe he could sense her panic, or perhaps he didn't like the hiss in her voice, but Archie began pushing against her arms.

'It's okay, Buttons,' she whispered, trying to reassure him.

But it was too late. Bending away from her, he lunged towards Charlie across the table. Charlie caught him, and she watched, mute with remorse, as Archie curled his small arms around his brother's neck like the toy monkey he was clutching.

It was what she'd dreaded happening most of all—and now she had made it happen.

Pain knifing her chest, she spun away and began walking blindly towards the lush, flower-filled garden. Vast pine trees created shady pathways, and within minutes she could no longer see the house. Without the rush of adrenaline her feet began to stumble and slow, and she stopped in a light-dappled clearing.

Through the trees she could see stripes of blue

ocean. The air was heavy with the scent of flowers and the tang of salt and it was quiet—even quieter than the house. Suddenly she had never felt more alone.

Her eyes blurred with tears. She missed Della so much. Her sister had always made her feel safe and strong. Not small and stupid.

A twig snapped behind her and, turning, she felt her breath stumble in her throat.

Charlie was standing at the edge of the path.

'Dora—'

'Where's Archie?'

'He's fine. Shengyi is reading him a story.' He paused. 'Look, Dora—'

'Why are you here? You've got what you wanted so just leave me alone.'

'You think this is what I want?' Frowning, he walked swiftly towards her. 'I'm trying to help—'

'Yourself,' she interrupted shakily. 'Not me. You're just trying to make me look useless so you can take Archie away from me.'

'I'm not.'

As she started to turn, he caught her arms.

'Maybe before that was true. But not now. Not since I've seen how much he needs you.'

His words echoed dully in the sunlight, and she shook her head. 'That's not true.'

It was the other way around: she needed him.

Only at some point in the future there were going to be weeks, maybe even months, when Archie would be here in Macau and she would be alone.

Yes, she was his guardian at the moment, so she could simply refuse to let Archie see his family here. But that would be wrong...selfish.

A tear slid down her cheek, followed by another, and then another. 'He puts up with me because I'm all he's got. But he's not happy.'

She pushed against Charlie's chest, slamming the flats of her hands against the solid pectoral muscles, directing her anger at him.

Only he wasn't to blame.

A sob caught in her throat as her hands stilled. 'And that's my fault.'

For a moment Charlie just stood there. Her distress hurt his chest much more effectively than her hands. He could feel her despair deep inside, as if it was his own. She was hurting—missing her sister...grieving.

He felt shocked at his stupidity. Of *course* she was grieving. But, truthfully, he hadn't meant to upset her. He had expected her to kick against the idea of a nanny, but not to burst into tears.

'As long as you get what you want you'll do or say anything.'

He flinched inwardly as Dora's accusation ricocheted round his head.

In the past that had been true, but right here and now, with her, he didn't want to be that man, and as she continued to cry he pulled her against him. He felt her momentary resistance and then her body softened in his arms and he stroked her head, speaking quietly in Cantonese until little by little she began to grow calmer.

'It's not your fault,' he said, switching back to English.

He felt her take a shuddering breath.

'But it is. I don't know what I'm doing half the time, and Archie knows that. I think he's scared.'

'Of course he's scared.' He didn't like hearing that bruised note in her voice, knowing that he was partly responsible for it. 'And confused, and probably angry too. How could he not be? He's a baby and he's just lost his mother. His whole world, everything he's ever known, has changed.' He hesitated, and then gently tipped her chin up. 'Except you.'

Her grey eyes were swollen, and her cheeks

were smudged with mascara, but he saw with relief that she had stopped crying.

'You're still here. You're his constant. And you're doing a wonderful job.'

'If you believe that, why have you hired a nanny?'

'Shengyi is here to help, not to replace you.' He stared down at her, caught in the trap of her tangled blonde hair and parted pink lips. 'That wouldn't actually be possible,' he said softly. Reaching out, he ran his finger down her face. 'I don't think you could be replaced.'

Beneath the pounding of his heart he could hear alarms going off in his head, but they made no sense—not when she was so close that he could feel the soft curve of her breasts through his T-shirt.

'I've ever met anyone like you,' he said.

There was a beat of silence. He just had time to catch the flicker of heat in her grey eyes and then she took a step closer and her mouth fused with his.

This is a mistake on so many levels, he told himself.

But he didn't care.

The scent of her skin was filling his head and, unable to stop himself, he kissed her back, his lips and tongue urgent, pulling her closer, moulding her body against his. Her lips were soft, and she tasted sweet and warm like melting sugar. He felt her hand slide up over the muscles of his back and, framing her face, he deepened the kiss, wanting more of her sweetness.

His body felt hot and hard, like something forged in a fire. She was moving against him, her bare legs sliding between his so that the hard ridge of his erection was pressing into the soft mound of her belly. He felt light-headed with desire. Capturing her hair in his hand, he tipped back her head, his mouth seeking her throat, his hands sliding beneath her top.

She felt so good. Her skin was warm and soft, like suede. Suddenly exhilarated at being free to explore, he ran his hands over the contours of her body, his fingers bumping over her ribs, up to the underside of her breasts—

'Charlie…'

She whispered his name, but it was enough to drag his brain out of neutral.

What was he playing at? Had he lost his mind?

His head was still spinning at the speed and intensity of his desire but, ignoring the protests from his body, he stepped away from her and stared down at her face.

Her eyes were wide and unfocused, and she looked as dazed as he felt. 'I don't know how that happened...'

How was unimportant. What mattered was that it didn't happen again.

Glancing down at her flushed face, he felt his stomach tense.

Dora was his passport to Archie. Messing around with her wasn't just playing with fire—it was like dancing on the edge of a volcano. He was appalled at himself for letting things go so far.

He held her huge, stunned eyes with his. 'I take full responsibility.'

Her mouth twisted. 'I kissed *you.*'

'And I kissed you back. But I shouldn't have done. I wouldn't have done it, but you were upset.'

'Upset!' She stared at him and frowned. 'Are you saying you felt sorry for me?'

Before he could answer, her lip began curling up in shock and fury.

'Thanks, but I don't need your pity.' She was trembling.

'That's not what I meant. It's been a difficult few days. Your emotions are running high...'

'So now you're blaming me?' Her eyes narrowed. 'What happened to "I take full responsibility"?'

'Leave it, Dora,' he ordered.

Watching her chin jerk up, he knew his tone had been too sharp, but he didn't need to make a bad situation worse by engaging in some futile post-mortem on her impulsiveness and his lack of restraint.

'Just go back to the house and check on Archie.'

For a pregnant moment she stared at him in silence, and then she turned and stalked back the way she'd come.

He didn't watch her leave. Instead he took a breath and began walking in the other direction, before he could do anything else that might ruin his chances of keeping his promise to his father.

Like following her.

CHAPTER FIVE

IT WAS A beautiful day.

Shielding her eyes from the sun, Dora shifted lower on her lounger. In front of her, the mirror-smooth surface of the oval-shaped swimming pool beckoned like an oasis in the desert. Beside her chair, the ice was melting in a tall glass of mango-and-coconut smoothie.

In another lifetime this would be a near-perfect afternoon, she thought, looking up into the cloudless blue sky.

Unfortunately every silver lining had a cloud. And in this case the cloud was about six feet tall, with intense dark eyes and a jawline you could lathe wood on.

She glanced furtively over to where Charlie stood in the pool, holding Archie. She felt her heart contract. The baby was pounding the water with his fists, his little face rapt with excitement beneath his sun hat.

He looked adorable. She must get a photo, she

thought, picking up her phone. But as she gazed at the screen she felt the muscles in her back tense.

All through breakfast and for most of the morning she had studiously avoided looking at Charlie. Now, though, thanks to the magic of modern technology, she could see him unfiltered and close up, and her fingers twitched against the phone, moving of their own accord to zoom in on him.

Her mouth dried. Yesterday she had imagined what he'd look like naked. Now she knew.

Her eyes drifted hungrily over the smooth skin of his back and the sweeping muscles of his shoulders. He looked as good as he'd felt. Her heartbeat accelerated, and before she had a chance to edit her thoughts she was back in that clearing, with her body pressed against the solid wall of his chest, the pulse between her thighs pounding in time to the ocean waves.

Remembering her hunger, her eagerness, she breathed out unsteadily, a flush of heat rising up over her throat and face.

It would have been so easy to surrender to that hunger. She had been lost in the moment…her pulse chasing his fingers as they'd slid over her body, shaping and sharpening her desire.

She had kissed men before, but she had never remembered any of those kisses. Not like this. Not like with Charlie.

She felt as if she was at one of those art installations where a video played on a loop, so that she could watch and re-watch every single second from that moment she had leaned into him right up to when he had called a halt.

She felt a prickling sensation and, refocusing on her phone screen, she felt her stomach flip. Charlie was staring over at her, his dark eyes magnified so that for a moment it was as though he was right there in front of her.

'Can you turn Archie towards me?' she managed. 'He's looking the wrong way.' Cheeks burning, she made a show of framing the shot. 'Thanks.'

Leaning forward, she pretended to play with the picture while her face cooled. She might have found their kiss memorable, but he hadn't. Or, more likely, judging by the way he had reacted yesterday, he simply wanted to forget his lapse of judgement.

Her cheeks reheated. He had wanted her at the time. Even without the hard, insistent press of his erection, she knew enough about men to know that he had been aroused. And there had been a breathless, almost feverish urgency to his touch. His hands, his mouth, had been oddly clumsy, as though he had not been in full control of himself.

But any exultation she'd felt in his arousal had been short-lived. Whatever had burned in his eyes moments before—whatever she had imagined burned there—had been swiftly extinguished. And his reaction had confirmed that some of what had taken place, had taken place only in her head.

She felt her face get hotter.

He'd dismissed her—sent her back to the house as if he was a rock star and she some over-enthusiastic groupie. She had checked on Archie, put him down for a nap, and then read in her room until he'd woken up. Coming downstairs, she had somehow managed to sound polite and yet avoid meeting Charlie's eyes.

If he had noticed any coolness in her manner he'd made no reference to it. Instead he'd strolled in for dinner, looking cool and relaxed and basically as if they *hadn't* been chewing each other's faces off a few hours earlier.

And it had been the same this morning.

Oh, she felt so stupid. It was embarrassing enough that she had kissed him, but it was mortifying knowing that he classified what had happened between them as a narrow escape.

Hypocrite, she thought.

She felt the same—she just didn't want *him* to feel it.

But they were both right. Whatever it might have felt like when he had held her, it had just been a trick that intimacy had played on her senses, and that was the reason why she had never let things get this far with anyone before now.

Sex—at least the one-night stand variety—was different. That was sex on *her* terms. But anything more and the rules said that you had to share more of yourself than your body.

Only how could she do that?

She couldn't let someone see the 'real' her—couldn't face them discovering that she wasn't worth keeping. Or loving. And so she had always stopped herself before anything could get started. Not getting started equalled not getting hurt later down the line.

Her jaw clenched. Pity she hadn't remembered that yesterday.

But it wouldn't happen again. She was done with giving away pieces of herself just to get half of nothing back.

'Do-Do.'

Looking up, she blinked. Charlie was standing beside her, holding Archie against his sun-dappled torso. With the sun behind him, she couldn't read his expression, but she could feel his eyes skimming over her skin like two dark stones.

Being on stage had made her bulletproof regarding her appearance—but then she had never had to sing wearing an electric blue bikini, and suddenly she wished she had chosen to wear a one-piece instead.

'Hey, Buttons.'

Smiling, she took the baby onto her lap and began drying him gently with a towel.

'He's very confident.'

Her heart jumped slightly as Charlie dropped down onto the lounger beside her. He had smoothed his wet hair back against his skull and, averting her eyes from the droplets of water trickling down his shoulders and chest, she said quickly, 'He's been going to Tadpoles—it's a baby swim class. He absolutely loves it; he always loved it—even the first time, when some of the other babies got upset.'

Without thinking, she smiled at the memory—

and then felt her stomach clench as Charlie's eyes dropped to her mouth.

'What made you think of taking him?' he asked.

'What?' She frowned. 'Oh, it was Della's idea...'

Something pinched in her chest and she lowered her face, brushing her cheek against Archie's damp hair. Tears formed behind her eyes. She could still remember sitting at the side of the pool, watching her sister's face, seeing her absolutely fierce pride and love and thinking how lucky Archie was to have Della as his mother.

'It's in his nature to be brave,' Charlie said gently. 'To try new things.'

'Why do you say that?'

Reaching out, he picked up the toy monkey and held it out to Archie. 'He was born in the Year of the Monkey. That makes him smart and brave. And a little bit of a show-off.'

He smiled then, his mouth curving up like the petals of a flower opening, and Dora felt her pulse accelerate. It was the first time he'd smiled like that, and a part of her hoped it wouldn't be the last.

Unsmiling, he had a beauty that was intimidating, but when he smiled it made her want to reach out and touch the corners of his mouth, press her thumb—actually her own mouth—against the fullness of his lips.

Great idea—and then you can make an even bigger fool of yourself.

Archie gave a squawk and, realising he had dropped his toy, she was relieved—grateful, even—to close herself off from that particular memory.

Leaning over, she picked it up. 'So that's why you gave him this. Are you a monkey too?' she asked.

His eyes rested on her face. 'A tiger.'

She glanced up at his hair. Of course. Although he didn't need the stripes, she thought. There was an inner stillness to him that reminded her of a big cat—the same unsettling mix of grace and beauty and power.

For a moment it was on the tip of her tongue to ask him about her sign. But she knew herself well enough to admit that she would probably end up looking it up online and trying to work out their compatibility, or something equally dumb—and, anyway, why was she even *thinking* this?

'Can I run something by you, Dora?'

'Maybe…' She could hear the uncertainty in her voice. 'Depends what it is.'

Great, now she sounded like a sulky teenager.

'I know this is a short trip, and Archie's not even a year old yet, but you are his guardian and I think it's important for you to get an understanding of the family business as soon as possible.'

She had thought he was going to suggest a family get-together with his half-sisters—not a business tutorial. She felt a ripple of panic. It was hard enough learning parenting skills—surely she didn't have to become a businesswoman, as well?

But this was Archie's legacy. She couldn't just close her eyes and pretend it wasn't there. She had to do what Della would have done and protect his interests.

'Are you saying you want to sit down and talk to me about it?'

He shrugged. 'We could certainly do that, if you would prefer. But I was thinking it might be easier to show rather than tell.'

She looked at him blankly. 'What does that mean?'

'I was hoping you might join me at the complex this afternoon. I can show you round...talk you through the day-to-day operation.' When she didn't respond, he frowned. 'Is that a problem?'

'No, not a problem.' She hesitated. 'It's just that after what you said in London I thought introducing Archie to his half-sisters was your priority.'

His dark eyes didn't leave her face. 'Unfortunately, that won't be possible,' he said slowly. 'They're visiting friends in New York.'

She wanted to ask, *So why was it so urgent that we come over right now?* But perhaps he hadn't known.

Charlie reached out and she felt her limbs turn to butter. And then he ruffled Archie's hair and a needle of embarrassment slid beneath her ribs as she realised her mistake.

'If you would rather talk about it here, we can spend the afternoon in my office,' he said softly.

An oscillating tingle scraped over her skin.

Spend an afternoon with Charlie. On her own. In his office. Probably with the door closed, so they weren't disturbed.

There was no way she was doing that.

'No,' she said quickly. 'You're right. It would be better to see it for myself.'

Two hours later, she was trying not to look as dazzled as she felt.

'Slot machines make up only zero point five per cent of our business,' Charlie said, guiding her through the gaming floor. 'Baccarat is the most popular game. But we offer Black Jack and Roulette. And Sic Bo.'

Dora frowned. 'What's that?'

'It's a local game. You have a fifty-fifty chance of winning.' He glanced across at the gaming tables. 'Understandably, it's very popular.'

Trying to close off the panic swelling in her chest, she nodded. She had been to Las Vegas for a hen weekend, so she'd thought she knew what to expect, but she had never seen anything like the Golden Rod.

It was close to being the biggest casino hotel in the world, and apparently once Charlie's plans for extending and refitting were finished it would dwarf its rivals.

That her beautiful little nephew—Della's baby boy—was going to inherit even a portion of its revenue made her head spin almost as much as the stunning glass ceiling and the museum-quality Qing dynasty porcelain.

Thinking about Della made her lose concentration. It was difficult to imagine that the man who had owned all this had been her sister's lover.

Archie's father.

He was going to be a very rich young man.

How long would it be before Archie succumbed

to the glamour and opulence? And it wasn't just the trappings of wealth. Here in Macau, he had a half-brother, half-sisters—a family.

In comparison, what could life in England offer him?

She bit her fingernail. The short answer was not much. One aunt, two indifferent grandparents and a small terraced house with a power shower.

'Now might be a good time to pause, perhaps have some tea,' said Charlie. 'I'm sure you have plenty of questions, so let's go somewhere quieter.'

At the word 'quieter', she felt her solar plexus squeeze. Tea would be lovely, but 'quieter' likely meant somewhere without people.

Keeping her face carefully expressionless, she said, 'Could we have it down here? So I can sample what's on offer?'

She felt as if she was playing poker, or perhaps chess. All this having to think ahead and see all the angles… But if Charlie suspected she was trying to avoid being alone with him, he gave no indication.

Less than five minutes later they were sitting in a beautiful, traditionally styled tea lounge.

They weren't exactly in the thick of it. The tables around them were conspicuously empty. But there were enough people around for her to feel safe.

Safe-ish, she thought, glancing to where Charlie was sitting, his mesmerisingly handsome face giving nothing away.

Even without the accompanying bodyguards, you could tell he was a VIP. His bespoke but determinedly inconspicuous suit signalled his status almost as much as his nothing-to-prove manner.

'Do you like it?' he asked.

'I think it's beautiful,' she said truthfully, gazing around the room at the polished mahogany furniture and bronze lanterns. Like his home, it paid homage to Chinese aesthetics, but not in a tacky or hackneyed way. 'It's got a real nineteen-thirties vibe.'

He smiled slowly, his dark eyes steady on her face. 'In the thirties, before Macau was the Vegas of the East, it used to be known as the Casablanca of the South China Seas.' Waving away the waiter, he leaned forward to pour the tea. 'It had it all. Opium smugglers. Smoky nightclubs. Gangsters on the run and beautiful women.'

The pupils of his eyes flared, and she felt the thick choke of desire in her throat.

'Basically, it was the original sin city,' he said softly.

Watching the faint flush of pink spread over Dora's skin, Charlie felt his body grow painfully hard. Right now, with an erection bulking out the front of his trousers, there were any number of rules he would break to pull Dora across the table and onto his lap.

She was wearing a silky blouse, and that skirt she'd worn in London the day this had all kicked off between them.

He had denied it at the time, but he knew he had never felt such all-consuming lust for a woman.

Obviously. She was forbidden fruit.

His brain paused, recalling that moment in the garden when he'd tasted her, and he felt desire tug at him again. He wanted to consume her— only it wouldn't be knowledge he acquired, but chaos and regret. Something he'd already emphatically proved by kissing Dora.

It was the first time in his life he could remember losing control to the point where he let desire cloud reason and sense.

But desire was not an excuse. There was no need to grab when the table was full. His father had drummed that into him when he was a small boy. And for men like him and Lao Dan the table was always full.

Acting otherwise would demonstrate a lack of self-belief his father wouldn't have countenanced in his worthy heir.

What Charlie needed was to get back into his routine.

Last night, he had slept badly. His body had felt as if it was in a vice. And seeing her earlier in that electric blue bikini hadn't helped either.

It wasn't only the memory of that kiss that had kept him awake. He couldn't forget the pain in her eyes. It was a pain he understood. A pain that stemmed from fear—fear of being pushed to the outer edges, where it was cold and dark and silent.

But Dora would be fine. He would make sure she was financially secure, for Archie's sake. This—this flirting, this pull-me, push-me between them—was going to stop now.

That was why she was here.

Here, surrounded by people, he was safe from the hunger and the longing. Or that was the theory.

Leaning back, he watched her blush fade.

'Sin and secrets,' she said finally. 'No wonder you fit in so well.'

He picked up his cup, letting the fragrant steam fill his nostrils. 'I told you before—I have no secrets.'

'And I suppose you've never sinned either?'

Not with you, he thought, unable to drag his eyes away from her teasing, grey eyes.

'What can I say? Law by name—law-abiding by nature,' he said softly.

'Nicely swerved.' She smiled. 'This place is wasted on you. You should be running the country.'

He held her gaze, transfixed by her smile. 'Who says I'm not?'

She shook her head. 'Okay, I fold.'

'That's pretty early in the game.'

'You forget…' She ran her finger along the rim of her cup. 'I work in a casino. I see what happens if you get out of your depth. Not that I'm comparing Blakely's to this. Or even to Vegas.'

'You've been to Vegas?'

Pushing a strand of hair behind her ear, she frowned. 'Why the surprise?'

'I didn't have you down as a gambler.'

'I'm not a gambler. It was a hen weekend.' She

wrinkled her nose. 'It was okay. Bit like a theme park. We had a private table on the first night, and then we spent the rest of the time by the hotel pool and in the karaoke bars.'

He watched her pick up her cup and glance away. She had covered it up quickly, but just for a second he had seen a flicker of panic in her eyes when she spoke, as though she had revealed something.

More than anything, he wished he knew what.

His guts twisted. His motive for bringing her to the casino was simple. He wanted to show her what he could offer his brother; make her see the benefits of accepting that he was part of Archie's life.

Now, though, he was getting distracted by her—not just the pretty face, but the woman. Maybe the pretty face too, he thought a moment later, watching her throat as she swallowed her tea.

'That's interesting,' he said.

She looked over at him, and gave him a small, mocking smile. 'Earth-shattering I'm sure.'

'No, really. I don't often get feedback from someone in your position.'

'You mean, low-paid and with no prospects?'

Unable to resist the gleam in her grey eyes he laughed. 'My turn to fold, I think.'

'I thought the house always won,' she said softly.

'Then you must be the exception to the rule.'

He felt a ripple of excitement glide beneath his skin. She was a warm-bodied, soft-mouthed exception to *every* rule.

With an effort, he dragged his mind away from that tempting image. 'So why would you prefer Macau to Vegas?' He didn't really care what she thought—he just wanted to direct the conversation away from the black ice of their banter and back to the solid ground of business.

She hesitated. 'This feels classier. More sophisticated.' Her gaze flicked over his shoulder. 'For starters, the female staff don't dress like they work in a nineteenth-century brothel.' A smile dimpled her cheek. 'I guess that's one of the many benefits of having sisters. Makes for a more enlightened man as a boss.'

Charlie felt his shoulders tense. Dora's innocent assumption of his familial closeness could hardly be farther from the truth.

Lei, Josie and Sabrina... He and his half-sisters all held positions in their father's empire and they all presented a united front to the world. They had to. That had been the price of admission to any relationship with Lao Dan. His father had demanded and enforced a façade of family unity and, raised since childhood to seek his approval, they had complied.

Only at what cost?

He reflected on the fierce bond of love between Dora and Della, then he pushed the thought away. Yes, his father's way had been unflinchingly ruthless, but so was life.

Only by training hard, by enduring tough lessons early on, could you deal with life. And not just deal with it, but triumph. Dora wouldn't get why it was important for Archie to learn those lessons too and nor did she need to: she had no place in his father's dynasty.

He shifted in his seat. 'This is supposed to be an opportunity for you to ask me questions. So, do you have any?'

There was a pause. The shadows under her eyes made her look young, uncertain.

'Did Della ever come here with him?' There was a quiver on the margins of her voice. 'Your father, I mean.'

'They worked together, Dora,' he said quietly.

'I know. I just wondered whether he went out with her...or whether it was just... Actually, never mind.' Her eyes found his. 'I'm sorry. That was a stupid, inappropriate question.'

So that was why she had looked so furtive earlier. She had been thinking about her sister. It was a testament to how distracted he was that he had forgotten Della had worked here. Or that Dora would make that connection.

His chest tightened. First rule of the casino: leave your emotions at the door.

And he always had. Until now.

'They were very discreet—so, no, I don't think they came here outside of work. But he cared for her. It was more than just—'

'Thank you,' she said quietly.

'For what?' He frowned.

'For answering me.' She screwed up her face. 'I know it must be difficult, talking to me about her…about them.'

It should be.

There had always been other women for his father, but none had given him a child—a son— and his mother had been devastated.

It had hurt, seeing her so upset, so diminished. But without their affair there would be no Archie.

No Dora.

'Excuse me, Mr Law.' His PA, Arnaldo, took a

step forward and bowed. 'I'm sorry to interrupt, sir. It's just that your sister Lei is on her way to your office.'

He felt Dora's surprise even before she started to speak. 'I thought you said they were away?'

'I thought they were.' The air-conditioned tea lounge felt suddenly oppressively warm. Turning back to his PA, he nodded. 'Thank you, Arnaldo. Shall we?' he asked, turning to Dora.

He stood up, waited for Dora to get to her feet and then he moved swiftly through the casino, guiding her past the tables.

Lei could wait. It wouldn't be important. Her turning up unannounced was just part of the long-standing pattern of their relationship—the incessant jockeying for position between siblings that had dominated all their lives.

Only pulling rank wasn't what had made him get up and leave...

His hand tightened against Dora's back.

He and his sisters put on a convincing demonstration of closeness, and up until a few minutes ago it had never bothered him that it was just a performance. But now he and Dora had shared a conversation of unscripted honesty—*his first*—and it seemed jarringly wrong to juxtapose the two, to taint such a genuine moment of trust and openness with something so elaborately false.

As they turned towards the exit she frowned, but without giving her time to speak he reached for her arm and propelled her through the doors and into his waiting limousine. Sliding in beside her, he released his grip.

She stared up at him, her face stiff with shock and confusion. 'I don't understand. I thought we were going to meet your sister?'

'You thought wrong.' He saw the harshness of his voice reflected in her eyes. 'Now's not the right time.'

It was certainly not the right place. To allow such a private, delicate matter to be aired in public would have most certainly provoked his father's cool-eyed displeasure.

'Why not?' She hesitated. 'You have told them we're here, haven't you?'

'Of course.'

'So why didn't you introduce me? What's the problem?' Now her eyes were looking directly into his.

'I don't have a problem.'

She frowned. 'Are you saying I do?'

'Judging by how you're overreacting right now, I would have to say yes.'

He knew he was being unfair. But he needed to take control of the situation, to shut down this conversation before it got out of hand.

'Look, Dora, I thought it would be obvious, but clearly I need to spell it out to you. It's not you they want to meet. It's Archie.'

That was true—but only in the sense that his sisters had almost certainly not given Dora a second thought. So what if she was the sister of their father's mistress? Their father had had many mistresses.

He wanted to close down this discussion.

Her eyes widened, and she flinched as if he'd slapped her. There was a short, impenetrable silence.

'Right. Of course. I...' Her voice trailed off.

In the rear-view mirror, he could see his driver's dark eyes staring fixedly ahead. Just for a second he thought about trying to explain. But Dora was already sliding as far away from him as possible and, glancing over at her stiff profile, he felt a mix of relief and frustration.

As soon as they arrived back at the house she was out of the car and gone before he even had a chance to turn and speak to her.

He left her to feed Archie and put him to bed and, left alone, retreated to his study and tried to distract himself with a game of mah-jong. But he kept seeing her face in the limo.

Why was this *his* fault? Anger clotted his throat. If she hadn't kept pushing…

Staring down at his desk, he noticed the report his security team had compiled on her and, pulling it closer, he flipped it open.

It was hard to remember a time when she had been just a name. His eyes focused on a photograph. It had been taken outside the nursery. Dora was holding Archie against her face, and his chubby hands were gripping her neck.

Gazing down at the photo, he felt his anger ooze away. For years he and his half-sisters had played the part of being one big, happy family. Maybe now, for Archie's sake, they should play it for real, he thought, pulling out his phone.

He found her in the library.

She was hunched in a chair, hugging her knees, staring down at a novel he knew she wasn't reading.

He sat down facing her, beside a pile of books. 'What I said in the car—it was insensitive and unnecessary.'

She didn't look up at him. 'And also true.'

'Not any more. I've spoken to my sisters.'

Her beautiful pink mouth twisted. 'Right. So you fixed it? Just like that? Problem solved?'

He thought back to the conversation with his sisters. It had been awkward at first, and yet there had been less of the usual feeling that they were duelling rather than speaking. It had made him think that had their father not played them off against one another, it might have been different. They might have got on, formed bonds, been friends as well as siblings.

Like Dora and Della.

'Not solved. Addressed. I can be persuasive when I want to be.'

He was trying to lighten her mood, but she didn't smile. 'It's not fixed, Charlie. Or solved. Or addressed. Because it's not your problem. It's mine.' Her fingers tightened around the book. 'You were right, before...about how I reacted.'

Remembering how *he'd* reacted, he felt a spasm of guilt. 'You're Archie's aunt—you were just looking out for him.'

'Yes but... Oh, what's the point? You wouldn't understand.'

Wouldn't listen...wouldn't care. It was an accusation his mother had thrown at him more than once. And it had been true with her. He'd had to pick a side, choose how to think, to act, to talk, and he had picked his father's way so that Lao Dan would see himself in his son.

That was what his mother had wanted—for him to be 'the golden child'—and he'd done it to please her.

Only what she hadn't got was that his choice had meant conditioning himself to treat emotion as weakness.

But he did want to listen to Dora, and he did care. 'Perhaps, but I'm willing to try,' he said.

'I don't know how to explain it,' she said slowly. 'It's just that since Della died it's been the two of us. Then you come along and Archie suddenly has this whole other family. I suppose I assumed I would be a part of it. Not the money and stuff—I don't care about that.'

'I know.'

She shook her head. 'It sounds pathetic.'

He looked at her still, tense body and then, reaching out, he gently turned her face towards his. Her hair was a mess, her cheeks were smudged with mascara, but she was beautiful.

Beautiful—and brave to admit her fear. A fear she had hidden from everyone, even those closest to her.

'It's not pathetic. It's perfectly natural. You're grieving, Dora. And I know you don't want to look like you're not coping, but it's okay to reach out for help. Talk to your parents, they'll understand.'

Do as I say, not as I do, he thought.

'My parents!' Her voice was taut, stretched like piano wire. 'Didn't your report tell you? You should probably ask for your money back.'

He felt his stomach knot. She had parents; they were divorced. What else was there to know?

'I only asked them to look into your current situation. Your past was irrelevant.'

'You got that right.' In the fading light, her knuckles glowed white. 'I was a mistake. My mum didn't love my dad any more. She was so desperate to leave him, she left me behind too.' She hugged her knees tighter. 'She walked out when I was a few months old, so I don't think I'll be reaching out to *her*. And as for my father, David—he stayed, but only for Della.'

'I'm not sure that's true.'

'And *I'm* sure that it is.'

The ache in her voice made his chest hurt.

'When I was little I heard him and Della arguing about me. He didn't believe I was even his. And then, when I turned out to be such a mess, I think he hoped I wasn't.'

'You're his daughter, Dora.'

She tried to smile. 'He left when I was thirteen—so, you see, I'm nobody's daughter. Della had to go to court to keep me. And she did. She took care of me. Even when I was a monumental pain.'

He didn't need to be in her skin to know how she felt. The difference was in how they had responded to the hard facts of their lives. She had curled into a ball, bristling like a hedgehog, whereas he had become a chameleon, endlessly adapting to each new situation so that he wasn't even sure who Charlie Law was any more.

He steadied himself against the thought. 'You were thirteen. Everyone is a monumental pain in the ass when they're thirteen.'

'But I was nineteen when I dropped out of university. Della had worked so hard so I could "follow my dream", and then I just threw it all away. I let her down. And now she's gone.'

The room was growing dark, and he reached out to turn on the lamp.

'Don't,' she whispered.

He could hear the tears in her voice, and his body reacted instinctively. Gathering her into his arms, he pulled her onto his lap. 'You didn't let her down. And now you're taking care of her son—my brother. That makes you part of my family. And I take care of my family.'

Her eyes lifted to his mouth and he felt a frisson of heat shoot through his body. She felt soft and warm in his arms, almost as if she was melting into him.

'Dora…' he said softly, mesmerised by her beauty. His voice frayed as she shifted against him. 'You're not… I want…'

'Want what?'

Her thumb twitched against his arm, and he felt suddenly light-headed with desire.

I want you. Except that didn't seem like something he could say to the beautiful woman on his lap—not when it might make her get up and leave. And he didn't want that to happen. Although he knew what mattered here was what *she* wanted.

She looked up at him and gently, with fingers that shook ever so slightly, traced the curve of his jaw. His heart was hammering against his ribs, willing her to go on, and yet he was taut with panic that she was going to call a halt.

'I want something that I shouldn't,' he said.

Breathing out shakily, she pressed her hand against the front of his shirt. Her grey eyes were soft and hazy, like a heat shimmer.

'What about if I want the same thing?' she asked.

He stared at her, mute with hunger, trying to resist her words. 'You're upset, Dora. You don't know what you're saying.'

'Then let me show you,' she whispered and, clasping his face in her hands, ran her tongue slowly along his lower lip.

CHAPTER SIX

FOR A MOMENT Charlie couldn't move. His head
was spinning. He could feel her trembling against
him as though she was cold. Only she wasn't
cold. Her skin felt hot and smooth to the touch,
and her warm breath was mingling with his.

His heart began beating faster.

He should stop this now.

He should ease her off his lap before they did
something crazy.

But why fight it?

Why keep denying the pull between them?

It was what they both wanted—had wanted
ever since they had first seen one another in the
lawyers' offices in London.

He felt his control snap and, moving forward,
pulled her body flush against his. Capturing her
face, he kissed her.

She leaned into him, her lips parting, and that
was all it took for his hunger to accelerate—the
tilt of her body, the taste of her mouth.

His hand tightened in her hair as he pushed his tongue between her lips and kissed her more fiercely. With one hand he lifted her to face him and she began moving against him, her hands clutching his shoulders as the pile of books slid to the floor.

Already his body felt as if it was made of iron, and the more she melted into him, the harder it got. He could feel her breasts through the fabric of his shirt, and he pulled at her buttons, parting her blouse.

Her bra was made of some kind of filmy white fabric and, gazing down at the dark outline of her nipples, he felt his head swim. Lowering his mouth, he caught one swollen tip in his mouth, feeling her arch towards him as he sucked it in.

But he wanted more of her. He wanted to taste her skin without the impediment of clothing, wanted to feel the curves and planes of her body. So he dragged the shoulders of her blouse down her arms, then her bra, baring her to his gaze.

She was staring at him, her grey eyes soft and drowsy with desire, her mussed-up blonde hair framing her beautiful face.

He breathed out unsteadily. Always with a woman there were certain steps, an understanding. This was different. It was the abandonment of his will to his senses—an irresistible pull in his blood like the gravitational draw of the moon on the ocean.

Reaching out, he let his thumbs skate lightly over her ribs, his mouth seeking the smooth skin of her neck, his tongue circling the pulse leaping at the base of her throat. Then he moved them down to her breasts, slowing the pace, taking his time, his hands gripping her waist, anchoring her to him.

Dora gasped. Her pulse was beating in her throat. Shock waves of desire were spreading out over the skin of her taut, aching body. His mouth was warm, the tongue curling over her nipple measured, firm, expert. She never wanted it to stop. Never wanted *him* to stop.

His hands tightened around her waist and she whimpered as he pulled her down, holding her against the thick press of his erection. Her stomach clenched. The ache that had started when his mouth had begun tugging at her breast was growing more intense, more decadent, so that she began to shake.

She had told him she wanted him. Up until now she hadn't realised how much. She wanted to touch his skin, run her fingers over the lines of his chest, her tongue down the fine line of hair along his flat stomach.

Her hands found his waistband, began to untuck his shirt. He lifted his mouth, his dark eyes swallowing her whole as she yanked his shirt open. She kissed him fiercely once, then again, and then, dragging her lips from his, ran her tongue down the side of his neck, her pulse jumping as shivers of anticipation twitched across his skin.

And then, trembling slightly, she laid her hand against the push of his erection.

His dark eyes were trained on hers.

'Dora, I—'

Shifting backwards, she slid between his legs to kneel in front of him. Her fingers worked the zip lower, and as she pulled him free of his trousers she heard him groan.

For a moment she held him in her hand, feeling the strength and the urgency beneath the taut silken skin, and then the desire to taste him overwhelmed her and she lowered her mouth, curling her tongue around him, drawing him into her mouth.

Charlie tensed, his body twitching, hardening fast, as Dora hitched her mouth upwards, inching forward, dipping her head back and forth.

He grew thick, then thicker still. He could feel his legs stiffening and he swallowed hard, fighting for control. With a groan, unwilling to climax too soon, he bunched up her hair and, gently lifting her head, took her mouth in a searing kiss.

Pulling her to her feet, he let his fingers find the button at her waist and, flicking it free, he slid her skirt down and hooked his hands into her panties. He drew her closer, his need for her beating feverishly in his blood as if they had no time.

And yet it felt as if they had all the time in the world…

He kissed the soft mound of her belly, then kissed a line down to where she was already hot and swollen, bringing her closer, then closer still.

He drew her panties away from her body, his breathing losing rhythm as he traced a path between the damp curls, gripping her thighs as she began to sway.

Dora breathed in sharply.

Her body was humming; she was growing dizzy. Her limbs felt light and she was losing all sense of herself. She clung to his shoulders, following the pulse of her hunger like gleaming white pebbles in the moonlight.

Around her the room seemed to be shrinking, growing smaller. Her whole being—every nerve, every cell—was centred on the tingling, insistent stroke of his tongue.

'Charlie…' She caught his hair, pushing him away and back onto the sofa, then reaching for him again, wanting to feel him inside her.

Her heart gave a lurch as he reached into his back pocket and pulled out a condom. Watching him smooth it onto his erection, she felt a ripple of shock. She had forgotten—would have forgotten in her haste, in her urgency.

But as his hands captured her naked body and he slid deep inside her she forgot everything. There was only the taut, steady strength of his hips as they pressed into her.

She felt herself swell, her body stiffening, pleasure rising inside her as he moved against her, filling her with heat, with a glowing heat that was growing whiter and brighter.

Reaching up, she clasped his face in her hands, her breath catching. She tried and failed to slow it down, and then she was arching against him, crying out as his mouth covered hers. He shuddered, his fingers pressing into her so that she couldn't tell where he ended and she began.

For a moment she lay against him in the half-light, her face buried in his chest, her muscles still gripping him, clenching and unclenching like a fist.

As his arm shifted against her back she felt a small pinch of regret. Not for what had happened here in this book-filled room. The sex had been good. In fact, she'd had no idea it could be that incredible. And Charlie was gorgeous—he knew how to touch, the pressure needed, how to change pace. He had made her pleasure his pleasure. Even now she could feel him deep inside her.

How could she regret that?

No, she regretted what *hadn't* happened. There were so many different ways to find pleasure, and she wanted to try them all with this man. Wanted to feel his weight on hers, to watch his eyes narrow with hunger as she straddled his body, his hands at her waist, holding her down…

A flint sparked inside her. She wanted to bend over on this sofa and feel him reach underneath her, to stroke the ache between her thighs.

She breathed out unsteadily. Her body felt waterlogged. She wanted to stay here for ever, pressed against the heat of his skin, with his hand twisted in her hair, and for a moment she let herself enjoy the feeling of intimacy, of skin on skin, and the comforting solidity of his body.

His lips brushed against her hair and she felt him withdraw, straightening away from her. She felt his gaze on her naked body, and suddenly her heart was racing.

Even in full sunlight it was impossible to read his expression. Here in the darkening room she could hardly make out his eyes. But maybe that was a good thing.

'What is it?' she said, hoping that the sudden thumping of her heartbeat wasn't audible to him.

'I was just thinking how very beautiful you are.'

It was the kind of thing lots of men said *before* sex—over dinner, in the pub, leaning in to shout it above the music in some club.

He hadn't.

Not so many of them said it afterwards.

And yet he had.

She glanced down her legs, dangling either side of his hips. It was that or look at him.

'You don't have to say that now.'

She didn't need any more reasons to think that Charlie was different from other men...special.

Leaning forward, he lifted a strand of hair,

twisting it around his finger. She sat still, breathing in the scent of his skin, and of herself.

'I'm not saying it because I have to,' he said softly, letting go of her hair. 'I'm saying it because I want to. And because it's true.'

His words felt good…almost as good as the feeling of his warm arm resting lightly against her back. But nothing good ever lasted. Not for her anyway. That was why she never stayed over—why she always moved on before anyone could get too close…close enough to see beneath the smile.

And that was why she had loved to sing.

Up on a stage there was always a distance between her and the audience. They saw and heard only what she wanted them to see and hear. It had been the one area of her life where she was—had been—in control.

Now even that was gone.

'We should probably get dressed…' She glanced past him at the door. Normally she would already be creeping through it. Once was always enough.

'Yes, we probably should,' he said.

But he didn't move to get up. He didn't even move his arm from her back.

'But what I *should* do and what I want to do seem to be at odds right now,' he said slowly.

Her breath scraped against her throat. So loud it seemed to fill the entire room. 'What do you mean?'

But she knew what he meant. And it felt as if something was tearing inside her.

Always before it had been easy for her to set boundaries, to walk away and not look back. Fear of getting hurt had outweighed desire and loneliness.

Della had known that, and had understood why she felt that way, but she had never judged or pushed her to change. And up until now Dora had never wanted to change—never felt any urge to let someone get close. She couldn't give someone the power to hurt her.

Only with Charlie she felt different. She wanted him more than she had ever wanted any man. And he had made her feel wanted, made her feel special.

But this was not the right time. He was not the man to let under her skin.

She glanced at her naked body. Maybe it was a little late to start worrying about it, but right now at least, everything was contained, confined to what had happened here in this room. It could still come under the heading of 'a bit of fun'—or even that most overused of clichés, 'a mistake'.

Her stomach twisted with panic. Except it didn't feel like a mistake. In fact it hurt her not to reach out and touch him.

'You know what I mean,' he said.

His voice was quiet, steady, and she felt herself grow calmer.

'This—you and me—is a bad idea. I know that logically, and yet I don't want to stop.'

She felt his dark eyes rest on her face.

'And I don't think you do either.'

She wanted to lie, to deny his words, but he was being honest with her in a way that reminded her of Della. Suddenly her breathing was snarled up.

Was this how it had started for Della with Lao Dan? Temptation disguised as truth? And then a tangle of feelings, shared and unrequited, ending with an unplanned pregnancy?

'I don't do relationships.' Lifting her chin, she leaned in slightly, wanting to see his reaction.

The tension between them was suddenly quivering like a telephone wire in a high wind.

'I don't do them either. But I wouldn't really classify what I'm offering as a "relationship".'

His hand flexed against her back as he spoke,

and she felt something inside her twitch in response. The room felt smaller, hotter.

'So what you want is some kind of "friends with benefits" arrangement?' she said slowly.

Had she actually said that out loud?

She felt his body harden beneath her and knew that she had.

'We don't need to overthink this, Dora. What I want is you. And you want me. It's been that way since I walked into that lawyers' office in London and you told me to keep my money.'

He shifted his legs, tipping her forward slightly so that she was forced to grab his shoulders to regain her balance. She felt her nipples brush against his bare chest and her abdomen tensed.

'I do want you,' she said. It wasn't fair of him to use her body against her. 'But, like you said, me and you…it's a terrible idea.'

Dipping his head slightly, he ran his tongue lightly over her lips and she breathed in sharply.

'Actually, I said "bad", not "terrible". And if we wanted different outcomes then, yes, that would be true. We would be pulling in different directions. But we want the same thing.'

He was right. She could feel the pull between them. Feel her body reacting eagerly, viscerally, to what he was suggesting even as it searched for tripwires in his logic.

'I want more of this, Dora,' he said softly.

She was silent, her mind racing in time to the pulse beating between her thighs. Again, she wanted to deny, to lie. In her experience the truth hurt too much to confront it. Only the truth here was that she wanted Charlie. And the idea of this being the last, the only time they had sex, hurt more than acknowledging that out loud.

And how would she get hurt anyway? She knew what was on offer. There were no unknowns. There would be no unrequited feelings or broken promises. No need to think beyond the bedroom—or the library. In fact, no need to think at all.

'I want more too,' she said slowly.

His eyes were suddenly dark and molten.

Yes, she thought.

And then his mouth was on hers and the time for thinking was over.

It was still dark when Charlie woke. Glancing down at Dora's sleeping body, he felt his breath catch low in his chest. She was curled on her side, her silky blonde hair fanning out over the pillow, her long dark eyelashes fluttering in her sleep. The skin of her cheek felt soft against his chest and, had he not been worried about waking her, he would have reached out and stroked it.

They had finally made it upstairs just after midnight.

There had been a moment, a few nerve-racking seconds, when he had thought the change of scene might change her mind about what they were doing. But as they'd reached the top of the stairs she had turned and kissed him so fiercely that it had felt like the most natural thing in the world to scoop her into his arms and carry her to his room.

His eyes fixed on her lips now, and he felt a beat of excitement pulse beneath his skin at the memory of what had happened both before that and afterwards. She had been so eager and un-inhibited. The memory of just how uninhibited was making him painfully hard.

His jaw tightened. He wanted her so badly it was making his teeth ache, but he wasn't about to wake her. Only neither could he lie next to her feeling like this.

Her arm hung loosely over his stomach and, lifting it carefully, he shifted free. He needed space to breathe, to think. His mouth twisted.

But not to overthink.

Pulling on the shirt and trousers he'd discarded last night, he made his way downstairs, drawn irresistibly to the library and to the traces of their encounter.

In an hour, his staff would start to rise, but for now he had the house to himself. And he needed that. Needed some distance between himself and the beautiful woman lying in his bed.

He blew out a breath, cooling his mind. There had been plenty of beautiful women in various beds on multiple occasions. But not *his* bed.

Why was she in his bed?

His eyes scanned the book-lined walls. The library was cool and quiet; he found it difficult to believe that just a few hours ago he'd had sex with her in this room, on that sofa. Not once, but three times.

Three times.

So why was she in his bed?

But it was no easier to answer that question the second time than it had been the first. All he knew was that this 'more' was apparently an endless pit of need and desire that he had never felt for anyone. However intriguing he'd thought a woman, he'd always found that sex solved the mystery.

So what was it about Dora that left so many questions unanswered?

Glancing over to the armchair, he thought back to the moment he'd found her. She had been upset over what he'd said about meeting his sisters. But of course what was really upsetting her was losing her own sister.

He gritted his teeth. Had he known how close they were? No, not really. Della had been a very private person, and they had never had much to do with one another—perhaps consciously on her part.

He did know that she had been exceptionally good at her job, and up until he had learned about her affair with his father he had liked and respected her quiet professionalism.

But from what Dora had told him last night she had been more than just a sibling to her younger sister. A lot more.

Hands tightening into fists, he stood up abruptly and walked to his study. The report was still on his desk and, picking it up, he flicked through it.

It was ironic. He had been so determined to find out some damaging facts that he had completely failed to notice the most important fact of all: her parents had abandoned her.

Nobody's daughter.

That was what she had called herself.

His chest felt leaden. His parents were flawed, but they had stuck around—not left him to be raised by an older sibling. At that age, could he have done what Della had done? *What Dora was now doing?*

Inside his head, he played back a fragment of last night's conversation—something about Della working hard so that Dora could follow her dream.

He frowned. Surely she hadn't dropped out of university to be a cocktail waitress. Flipping through the report again, he reread the part about her degree. She had been studying Vocal Performance.

Singing?

He hadn't expected that. And yet, like pieces of a jigsaw puzzle, words, remarks she'd made that had meant nothing on their own, were coming together to reveal an unexpected picture.

Reaching for his laptop, he typed in her name and stared down at the screen, his heartbeat accelerating. There were links to blogs and reviews—and videos. Clicking on one, he felt his mouth dry. It was Dora, her face pale in the spotlight, a little younger, with more make-up and glossier hair, but unmistakably her.

And she was singing.

He felt a head rush, his vision blurring, pulse dipping with shock. The venue might be unremarkable—some no-name club in London—but her voice…

His breath caught in his throat. Her voice was raw and distinctive…nerveless. She wasn't just talented, she had star quality—and that indefinable and, for most people, unattainable amalgamation of sex and swagger.

But she had given it up for Archie. Given up her dream.

Would he have done the same? Sacrificed his ambition?

His mouth twisted. *Unlikely.* To succeed—in other words, to earn their father's approval—he and his sisters had been pitted against one another in gladiatorial combat, and winning had been everything.

And yet yesterday that had changed. He had reached out to them and they had responded.

Shying away from all of the many disconcerting reasons why he had chosen to act like that, he closed the laptop. Beyond the window, the sun was just starting to creep through the trees.

Dora wanted to be part of Archie's life out here, and the more involved she felt, the more likely it was that she would agree to his half-brother returning to Macau on a regular basis.

The thought that she and Archie would soon be going back to England made something fray a little inside Charlie. He didn't want them to leave. 'Them', because, obviously, they came as a pair.

His heart was suddenly beating a little faster. But why did they need to leave so soon? Or even at all?

The idea burrowed inside him, and then it started to fizz like a sparkler, sending out showers of brilliant light into the darkness.

He wanted Archie to stay.

Archie needed Dora.

Dora needed to feel she belonged.

And, incredibly, he knew the perfect way to give her the security she craved.

More importantly, if he could get her to agree to what he had in mind it would make her, and therefore Archie, stay here in Macau for good.

'Do-Do! Do-Do!'

Rolling over, Dora felt the bed dip and, opening her eyes, started to laugh as Archie clasped her face with his hands and kissed her clumsily.

'You're all sticky.'

'Sorry, that's my fault.'

Glancing up, she felt her pulse stumble. Charlie was sitting on the edge of the bed—*his bed*—his dark eyes steady on her face.

'He ate some mango. I tried to clean him up, but—'

'He hates that,' she said quickly.

'He made that clear, but we got past it.'

Reaching over, he caught the little boy's foot and tickled him until he was screaming with laughter. She was astonished by how quickly and easily Archie had accepted Charlie into his life.

There was a knock on the door.

'I thought you might like breakfast in bed,' he said, standing up, his gaze meeting hers. 'I hope you're hungry. I know I am.'

Watching him cross the room and return with a breakfast tray, she fixed her eyes on the stretch of muscles beneath his shirt and felt her stomach somersault. It didn't seem possible that she could want him again, and yet she could feel her hunger for him almost swallowing her whole.

'Right—come here, little monkey.' Leaning

forward, he scooped Archie up in his arms. 'Time for your nap. Say goodbye to Dora.'

She felt her heart squeeze as the two brothers left. The rapport they shared felt less of a threat now. On the contrary—she knew it was a good thing. Charlie had a calmness that Archie clearly responded to.

Maybe she did too. Although not in the same way, she thought, her skin tightening as Charlie walked back into the room.

For breakfast there was fried rice, steamed buns filled with delicious vegetables, fresh fruit and sugar-dipped, deep-fried, stick-shaped doughnuts. It was all delicious.

'I don't know why I'm so hungry,' she said.

Their eyes met, and she bit into the smile curving her lips.

'Maybe I do.' He brushed something off her cheek and then, leaning forward, kissed her softly on her mouth. 'You taste of sugar.'

She felt her stomach drop. He tasted like pleasure and possibility all mixed up.

'Are you okay with this?' he asked softly.

That directness again. But, instead of scaring her, she found it reassuring that he was so forthright. This way there was no chance of any confusion, and it was the only way she would be able to let her herself wake up in his bed.

She nodded slowly. Before, with other men, she'd put up barriers, walking—running—from any hint of intimacy or commitment. But that wasn't a problem with Charlie. This would be a fling, and that suited them both.

'I never finished telling you what I spoke about with my sisters.' His dark eyes were level with hers. 'We got a little sidetracked.'

'So what did they say?' Her heartbeat accelerated. Had it really slipped her mind?

'It's Archie's birthday on Friday, so I thought it might be a nice idea to invite everyone over for a party.'

A party! She felt something twist in her chest. He had been serious, then, about fixing things.

She smiled. 'That would be lovely.'

'If you have any ideas, anything you think he might like, just let me know and I'll get someone to sort it out.'

It was stupid, but she could feel bubbles of happiness rising and popping inside her. Okay, the party was for Archie, but Charlie was holding it here, including her in the arrangements.

'Thank you. Is there anything I can do to help?'

His dark eyes rested on her face. 'There is one thing. None of us can hold a note, so I was hoping you might be prepared to sing "Happy Birthday".'

She stared at him in silence, the lightness of moments earlier seeping away, panic rising in her throat. She felt suddenly naked, in a way that had nothing to do with the fact that she wasn't wearing any clothes.

Sing. In front of people. In front of strangers. In front of Charlie.

A cold mass of dread was slithering from one side of her stomach to the other. She could remember it now; how the silence had seemed to seep into her through her open mouth. It had been like drowning…or suffocating.

'Is that okay, Dora?'

She felt Charlie's gaze on her face. She was being stupid. It was just singing 'Happy Birthday'. Obviously she could do it. She would do it for Archie.

With an effort, she forced her mouth into a smile. 'Of course. Although, you might have to write me the words phonetically if I'm going to sing it in Cantonese.'

He seemed pleased. 'Thank you. Usually we

hire a professional singer for parties, but it seems a bit over the top—and, anyway, we already have you.'

Her insides tightened. 'What do you mean?'

'I watched a couple of videos of you.' He hesitated. 'You're good. Very good.'

She couldn't speak. To speak would mean having to explain, and she couldn't explain without losing control. She'd done that twice already.

'I haven't sung in a while.'

'I know. You've had to put Archie first.'

She felt suddenly sick. *No, don't do that*, she thought. *Don't make me out to be some kind of saint.*

'What is it?'

He was frowning. Perhaps some of her feelings were showing in her face.

With an effort, she managed to smile. 'It's nothing. I just feel a bit odd about being centre stage. I don't really have the right to be there. I mean, it's a family party, and I'm not exactly family.'

His eyes rested on her face. 'You could be.'

She looked at him, startled and confused by his words. 'What do you mean?'

'I was thinking,' he spoke casually but there

was something in his voice that made her body tense, 'we could get married. Then you would be my wife, and part of the family. You would have every right to be there. To always be there.'

She felt as if the world had tilted on its axis. *Married.*

'Look, Dora… You being here works. You and I…we have an attraction—'

'It's sex, Charlie,' she said flatly. 'It's hardly a reason to get married.'

'It's incredible sex. I've never wanted a woman like I want you. I thought it would stop—that I'd stop feeling like this…' He stared past her, as though looking for an explanation. 'But it hasn't, and I haven't. And you feel the same way.'

Her heartbeat stilled as heat rushed through her, her body responding to his words. It was true. Her hunger for him seemed to be gaining potency and it was so tempting to let that mean something.

'And that's the reason you want to marry me?'

'Not the only reason, no.'

Her heart began to thump, and she could feel something flickering to life inside her—dry tinder catching fire. Was he talking about love?

'What matters is Archie, and you being here

works for him. This, just makes marriage a workable option.'

She blinked. Inside her, the flickering flame died.

His hand caught hers, and the strength in his fingers briefly made her forget the craziness of what he was suggesting.

'It wouldn't work.'

'It *is* working,' he said softly. 'And, more importantly, it's what my father and Della both wanted.'

'What? For us to *marry*?' She shook her head. 'I don't think so.' Her throat pulled tight as his eyes locked with hers.

'They wanted Archie to feel at home in London and here in Macau. If we marry, we can make that happen. For them—for him.'

Dora stared at him in silence. Marriage was not something she'd ever considered for her future. For Della, yes, but not for her.

His fingers tightened around hers. 'I'll make it work, Dora,' he said softly. 'I can take care of you and Archie. I can give you everything your heart desires.'

She felt her chest tighten and burn. *Not everything.*

But, then again, what was there left in England

for her? No family—or none that cared—a house filled with memories, a job she hated.

Now Charlie was offering her a new future. Financial security, a lifestyle most women could only dream of having and the best sex she'd ever had—probably would ever have.

Sex and security. Was that enough to make a marriage work? What about love?

She felt her heart start to thud against her ribs. *What about it?*

No one but Della, and now Archie, had ever loved her, and she loved Archie so much—more than enough to see past the craziness of Charlie's suggestion to the truth in his words.

And, anyway, maybe love was a bad idea in marriage. It certainly hadn't made her parents or Della and Lao Dan stick together.

Her heart squeezed.

It was a big decision. She should think about it—sleep on it, even. But she knew that until she'd made up her mind she would never be able to sleep again. And thinking that made it suddenly easy to say, 'Okay, then. I'll marry you.'

His eyes were dark, steady, unblinking. 'We can talk it through…make sure we're on the same page,' he began.

But she didn't want to talk. Instead she sat

up straight and let the sheet fall away from her body, knowing how he would react, needing to see him react.

And as he reached out to pull her closer she surrendered to his touch, breathing in the warmth and the scent of him, letting the desire ripping through her body blank her mind to the fear that it was not Archie's happiness but her hope of being wanted that had made up her mind.

CHAPTER SEVEN

IT WAS ANOTHER beautiful day. The perfect day, in fact, for the perfect first birthday party.

Shading her eyes, Dora glanced up at the cloudless denim-blue sky. She could hear the steady murmur of bees, and beneath the drowsy insect hum it was just possible to hear the distant soft swell of the ocean.

If only she could swallow the serenity of her surroundings, she thought, staring across the lush garden at a huge fig tree. Buddha had supposedly found enlightenment sitting beneath the branches of just such a tree, but she doubted it would do much to soothe her panicky thoughts.

She sighed. It was her own fault she was feeling like this. Less than a week ago Charlie had been her enemy, then her lover, and now here she was—not just having sex with him, but accepting his proposal of marriage.

Her heart gave a loud thump.

At the time, saying yes had felt like the right

thing to do. Right for Archie. And of course that was what mattered here. But she felt so unprepared.

The little she knew about real-life marriage was second-hand—mostly from David, about the unsatisfactory nature of his brief but disastrous liaison with her mother.

Her shoulders stiffened, her body tensing as it always did when she thought about her parents. Had it been their scant, imperfect love that had led her along this path to a marriage of convenience?

But today she wasn't going to let herself think about them, and why they'd always made her wish she was someone else.

She felt her heartbeat accelerate, and all thoughts of her parents were forgotten as Charlie walked out into the sunlight.

'Is everything okay?'

He stopped beside her, his dark hair falling silkily over his forehead, and she nodded, her mouth suddenly dry.

In the past she had wanted things—clothes, mostly—and when she was a teenager she had wanted boys in the sense of having a crush on them. And, briefly, whatever and whoever she had wanted had seemed extraordinary.

But once she had worn the dress, or kissed the boy at some party, that feeling of nervous anticipation had melted away like frost on a spring morning, so she had supposed that the same was going to be true with Charlie. That she would get used to him—to the devastating impact of his beauty.

Now she wasn't sure that would ever happen.

'Everything's fine. I was just thinking about the party,' she lied. 'About what to wear.'

It wasn't a complete lie. Last night, when Charlie had been putting Archie to bed, she had tried on every single item of clothing she had brought to Macau and each one had looked worse than the one before.

The blue embroidered kaftan she had thought looked bohemian in London looked shabby and badly made, the white shirt dress made her look like an off-duty nurse, and the striped jumpsuit she had been planning to wear had just brought back memories of those first few weeks of Archie's life last year, when Della had been so excited and full of plans for the future.

When Della had been alive to be excited about anything.

But today was Archie's birthday. It was supposed to be the happiest of days. A day of celebration and joy. And Dora would make sure that it was all of those things. Only, for her, it would be as much about what, or rather who, wouldn't be there.

And not just today. This was the first of many milestones her sister would never get to see. More than anything she wanted to do it right—the way Della would have wanted it done—and that meant presents and cake and blowing out candles.

And singing 'Happy Birthday' to Archie.

Her throat tightened against the panic that had been flapping helplessly inside her chest like an injured bird ever since she'd agreed with Charlie that she would sing at the party. She could sing under her breath, at home, and on her own with Archie—but even thinking about singing in front of other people made her want to throw up.

She knew she was being stupid—it wasn't as if she was about to go on stage in front of an audience of screaming fans—but it didn't seem to make any difference, telling herself that.

'Maybe we should go upstairs. You could give me a preview,' said Charlie, the pupils of his eyes flaring. 'It might help you make up your mind.'

His fingers moved up her arm, his thumb catching the side of her breast, and she felt her skin catch fire. Until Charlie, she had never known that just being close to someone could hollow her out with longing. Or that the lightest touch of a hand—*his hand*—could make warmth fill that hollowed-out space.

'That's why you want to go upstairs? To help me choose what to wear.'

She smiled, and after a moment he smiled too.

'I don't need to go upstairs to do that.'

His arm curled around her waist and her heart jumped.

'As far as I'm concerned you should wear as little as possible—nothing at all, preferably.'

She laughed. 'I think your sisters are going to have enough of a shock when they find out we're getting married without me turning up naked.'

They had decided to tell his family at the party, and agreed on their story. It was a tweak on the truth: they had met through Archie and fallen instantly and deeply in love.

Charlie seemed unfazed by how they might react and, although she thought he was being a little optimistic, she was distracted enough by the thought of singing not to care.

She met his gaze. 'Besides, I get to choose who sees my body, and some of me is only for you.'

His eyes darkened. 'All of you is only for me,' he said softly.

All of her? Was he saying he would mean his marriage vows? Take her for better or worse?

Her heart beat raggedly. Could she tell him about the fear that had gripped her that night in the club? The shame she felt at throwing away a dream that had required Della to make so many sacrifices?

But of course he wasn't talking about her as a person. He was talking about her body. Her agreeing to marry him didn't mean she could share with him what went on in her head.

He wasn't going to be that kind of husband.

Besides, she'd already confided in him way more than was necessary or appropriate.

Not that he had made her feel that. On the contrary, he had been sweet about her crying all over him.

But that was reason itself not to let it happen again. She had already got in deeper with Charlie than she had with any other man.

Never mind getting married—she had already let him hold her close enough to hear the beating of his heart, and that had been stupid, reckless.

She felt her stomach lurch.

Stupid because it had made her feel special.

Loved. Reckless because she knew how vulnerable she was to wanting someone—anyone—to feel that way about her.

But Charlie didn't love her. And if she was stupid enough to forget that fact, then she should remember his motives for proposing.

Maybe he had remembered too. Easing his grip, his voice no longer soft but casual, he said, 'So why can't you decide what to wear?'

She rolled her eyes. 'I can't believe you're asking me that. You have sisters. You should know women *never* have anything to wear. It's either too old, too tight, too boring…'

'Perhaps you need to get out of your comfort zone. Wear something different.'

'How? Are you going to rustle me up a couple of dresses?' She smiled. 'Is there no limit to your talents?'

The answering smile tugging at the corner of his mouth made heat stir inside her again, and she had to stop herself from leaning into him, letting her mouth find his and letting the tide inside her pull the feet from under her.

He stared at her steadily. 'Sadly, no to the first, and undoubtedly yes to the second.'

Not true, she thought, a faint flush colouring her skin as she remembered the way his hands and mouth moved over her skin, bringing the heat of his body into hers.

'Honestly, it's not a big deal. I never decide what to wear until the last minute.'

'Actually, it *is* a big deal,' he said quietly.

She stared at him uncertainly as he glanced away. Her throat had pulled tight so that suddenly it was hard to swallow, even harder to speak.

'What do you mean?' she asked.

'Look, Dora. What we talked about yesterday... I didn't actually think about what it would mean for you.'

Her heart felt heavy and cold with shock, but also with resignation.

Wow, that was quick.

But of *course* he wanted to bail. Everyone always did, sooner or later. Had she really thought he would be any different from the rest?

'That's very thoughtful of you. So is it just the party or is the wedding off too?'

'Off?' He frowned. 'No, that's not what I'm trying to say.'

It wasn't?

She felt the misery building in her throat start to unravel. 'So you haven't changed your mind?' she said slowly.

He shook his head. 'But we didn't really talk much about what it would actually mean.' His eyes rested on her face. 'There's more to my family than casinos and hotels. The Lao name is important in Macau. We have a certain standing. And that requires...' He hesitated, then held out his hand. 'Come with me. It will be easier to show you.'

'I don't understand.' They were standing in her bedroom, next to a rail of clothes. Dora was staring at the rail in confusion. 'Where did these come from?'

Charlie took a step closer. 'My sisters use a couple of stylists. I spoke to them yesterday and explained the situation.'

'I see,' she said slowly. 'And do you think maybe now might be a good time to explain "the situation" to me?'

'You came out here expecting to meet Archie's family and you packed accordingly.' He held her gaze. 'Only then we talked and things changed. I meant what I said about wanting to marry you. But I want you to feel comfortable doing that... being my wife.'

'Tracksuits are "comfortable", Charlie. This is Chanel.' Turning back to the rail, she pulled out a jacket, a silky skirt, then a beautiful embroidered dress. 'This is Dior...this is Gucci. This entire rail of clothes is probably worth more than my annual salary.'

'I know,' he said quietly. 'But this—' he gestured towards the rail '—this is what it means to be a Lao.'

He felt his breath tangle in his chest. It meant a whole lot more than that. It meant forfeiting ambitions, rights, boundaries. But to explain that would mean revealing much more than he was capable of sharing, and so, reaching into his trouser pocket, he pulled out a small square box.

'And this too.'

As he opened it, her eyes widened with shock.

'Look, Dora, this is how I live. All of this isn't optional. So I guess what I'm asking is...do you still want to be a part of that?'

She stared at him mutely and he felt his heartbeat accelerate at the thought of her refusing. From nowhere came something almost like panic that she wouldn't agree. Only, of course, that made no sense.

Finally, just as he was starting to think she would never respond, she nodded.

Taking the beautiful diamond ring, he slid it onto her finger. He thought about telling her that there was another reason he'd had the clothes sent over: because he'd wanted to do something to make her feel special.

Not that a few dresses could in any way make up for her parents' neglect, but he hated knowing that she had been hurt by them, that she was still hurting.

Her eyes met his, the grey soft but defiant. 'I won't need all these.'

'That's fine. Just choose what you like.'

She bit her lip. 'Sorry, that was rude. It's generous of you, and I am grateful.'

He felt something pinch in his chest. She was holding back for a reason he understood only too well. Despite his father's obsession with family unity, for most of his life being Lao Dan's son had felt like an ambition, not a birthright. And for Dora it was the same. Her caution was part of a learned pattern of behaviour never to take anything for granted.

He didn't know how to change that pattern—he just knew he didn't want to add to it.

'You don't need to be. Truly. You're part of my family now and, like I said before, I take care of my family.'

She looked up at him, and he saw some of the uncertainty fade from her eyes.

Reaching out, she ran a finger lightly over a silvery grey dress, the movement making it shimmer in the light. 'How did you know my size?'

She might as well have asked how he knew his own name. His hands had formed her, shaped her, followed every curve, mapped every line of her body to its edges, like an explorer uncovering a new world.

'I know everything about you,' he said softly.

It wasn't true. It wasn't even close to being true. But it made her mouth soften, her body turn towards his, and then, standing on tiptoe, she kissed him.

He could taste her hunger, and her hope, and just for a moment he almost wanted to push her away. It made him feel responsible—and, whatever he might have said about taking care of her, he didn't want to feel responsible.

But he could feel her need for him pulsing through her body into his, so he did what was natural and necessary.

Closing his eyes, he pulled her closer and deepened the kiss.

From somewhere inside the house Charlie heard the faint pop of a champagne cork, but he felt more as if a starter gun had just been fired.

His family had arrived. The party was starting.

As usual, his eldest sister, Lei, was first. Lei was beautiful, but had never been smart enough to fulfil Lao Dan's business ambitions. Instead he'd funded her moderately successful film career. What she liked best of all was taking centre stage at any family occasion.

His middle sister, Josie, was smart, with enough academic certificates to wallpaper all her homes across the globe. But she was also deeply insecure, and she had married a man who was both less successful and less intelligent than she was—a man their father had despised.

Sabrina, the youngest, was an entitled princess, indulged by both her parents. Work bored her, but she loved the benefits and the trappings of power that came with the Lao name.

None of them had anything in common except a surname and their father's DNA, but nobody would ever know that. Together, they were the Lao family. United, strong and—he glanced across to where dark-suited bodyguards scanned the garden through their sunglasses—bulletproof.

Nothing was more important than presenting that lie to the world.

Leaning forward, Charlie air-kissed his sisters in turn, and then nodded at their partners.

'So, where is he, then?' Sabrina frowned. 'Where's the birthday boy? Oh, what a sweetie—'

Breaking off, she made a cooing noise, and Charlie turned to follow her gaze, feeling his blood run cold.

Dora was standing behind him, with Archie in her arms. Her blonde hair was pulled into some kind of loose knot and she was wearing one of the dresses the stylists had sent over. It was white, with short sleeves and a collar edged with a deep band of pearls.

She looked beautiful; the perfect addition to the perfect family. It was easy to picture her standing beside him at the many events he and his half-sisters attended. And yet for some reason that picture pleased him less than the memory of her barefoot, wearing striped pyjamas and a scowl that could fell a Banyan tree.

Heart pounding, he watched her walk towards him. 'You look amazing,' he said as Archie reached out to grab him.

'Thank you. Sorry I took so long. He didn't want to wake up.'

'That's okay. You're here now.' He turned towards his sisters. 'Let's make some introductions.'

Everything would go exactly as he'd expected it would. How could it not? He and his sisters were accomplished performers. They knew exactly how to act, what to say and when to say it. And Archie was adorable.

But it was Dora who drew his gaze, and his admiration. She looked so beautiful, so determined.

'Everything okay?' he asked, moving to stand beside her.

She nodded. 'Thank you for making this happen.' Her eyes met his. 'Archie's lucky to have such a wonderful family.'

He should be pleased, he thought, and yet, looking down into Dora's face, he felt something knot in his stomach.

It had never bothered him before—the complicity between himself and his sisters. It had always been just a *sine qua non* for staying in his father's favour. Now, though, he felt less comfortable with the artifice of it all—and the fact that the layers of artifice and deceit were now multiplying to include Dora and Archie.

Suddenly he wanted it to be as it had before, just the three of them out by the pool, and with an urgency he'd never felt before he took her hand and pulled her slightly forward.

'As we're all here, it seems like the right time to share our good news.'

He felt her fingers tense.

Earlier, they had agreed to wait until Archie's cake was brought out to make their announcement. But he lifted her hand so that the diamond caught the sunlight and said quietly, 'I asked Dora to marry me, and she said yes.'

There was a moment of absolute silence and Dora held her breath. And then everyone began to clap.

Hardly daring to believe what was happening, she smiled and embraced first one then the other two sisters in turn.

She didn't need the glass of champagne Charlie handed to her. She felt intoxicated already—euphoric.

Only Della had ever known how much she dreamed of being part of a family. Not grudgingly tolerated, like she was by David, but accepted and included unconditionally. And now it had happened. These beautiful, poised people were raising their glasses and saying her name as if she was one of them.

'I think now might be the right time to do the cake,' Charlie said beside her. 'When you're ready, start singing and we'll join in.'

And just like that her happiness oozed away.

'Fine,' she said hoarsely, needing to say something—anything—so that she could hear her own voice.

It will be all right, she told herself. *There are only sixteen words, after all.*

More importantly, there were no strangers or spotlights. It was just a small family birthday party.

Archie's birthday party.

She glanced over at his little face, feeling a rush of love. His eyes were wide with excitement as Jian lit the candle on a beautiful monkey-shaped cake.

Her heart was pounding. In the sunlight, the flame looked oddly bright. Too bright. She tried to open her mouth—except it wouldn't open properly. It felt as if it was rusty, or something. And then the stiffness moved down her body as around her a silence like a held breath began leaching into her bones.

Archie.

She tried to turn her face, knowing that if she

could see his eyes it would be okay. Only he was staring transfixed at the candle.

But everyone else was looking at her.

In the blur of their faces she could feel their gazes drilling into her, sense their curiosity and, worse, their censure, and suddenly her heart was beating heavily, filling her chest so that it was difficult to find a breath.

She felt light-headed. Thin, sticky webs of darkness were clotting her throat, choking her, and then from somewhere close by she heard someone start to sing unfamiliar words to the most familiar tune in the world.

It was Charlie, his voice deep and assured. And then everyone was singing, and Archie was clapping, and she was forcing a smile, smiling until it hurt, wanting it to hurt, needing the pain to tamp down that other pain building inside her.

The rest of the party seemed to crawl past like a nightmare. She wanted to sneak away and curl up somewhere dark and private, but it was another hour before everyone left.

By then Archie was exhausted and, avoiding Charlie's eyes, she used that as an excuse to escape upstairs.

Archie was too tired for a bath, so she dressed him in his pyjamas and then, instead of putting him in his cot, took him to her bed and lay down beside him.

The ache in her chest felt like hot coals now. All along she had assumed that it was stage fright—the intangible, strangling fear of performing to an audience.

But there had been only eight people at the party—nine, including Archie.

It wasn't stage fright. And she couldn't blame her parents. She was the problem. She was always the problem—the reason why things failed. Her parents had seen that in her.

Her heart contracted.

Della had seen it too. That was why her sister hadn't made her Archie's guardian in her will.

She could tell herself that it had been an oversight, that Della just hadn't got round to sorting it out, but she knew deep down that there was only one explanation.

She closed her eyes against the hot sting of tears and the truth.

Della hadn't believed she could do it—hadn't trusted her to deliver when it mattered—*and she had been right.*

Look at this afternoon. All she'd had to do was sing to Archie on his birthday and she'd failed.

If she couldn't even manage that, how could she possibly raise him to adulthood?

Her body tensed. Across the room, she heard the door open—knew immediately it was Charlie, even before she heard his soft, firm tread. But she couldn't look at him right now; she wasn't sure if she could ever look at him again. So she kept her eyes closed, praying for him to leave.

She felt him reach past her and lift Archie, and even though she longed to keep holding his small, warm body against hers she knew she was being selfish. So she kept her eyes and her mouth shut.

The door closed and she breathed out shakily, but moments later the bed dipped beside her and she felt fingers—Charlie's fingers—gently stroking her face.

'Dora…'

She covered her mouth with her hand, holding her body tight with the other, trying to hold in the sobs.

'It's okay…' he said softly.

'No.' She shook her head. She couldn't bear the gentleness in his voice—couldn't bear anything any more. 'Just go, Charlie, please…just go.'

'I'm not leaving you like this—'

'But you will—' She choked on a sob, trying

to wipe away the tears that were streaming down her face. 'Everyone does—everyone leaves.'

'Not me. Not now. Not ever,' he said softly.

And suddenly he was pulling her into his arms, pulling her close, then closer still, holding her against the firmness of his body. She could feel herself responding to his warmth, could feel the old longing to be held arching like a glittering rainbow inside her.

She missed being loved so much, and she was so lonely. But she couldn't let that longing draw her in. Nothing would change the facts.

Pushing free of his arm, she shook her head. 'You were right before. He will have a better life with you.' She forced herself to look into his eyes, and then, before the ache in her heart could stop her from doing the right thing, she said quickly, 'I want you to have Archie. I want you to be his guardian.'

Charlie stared at her in confusion. It was what he'd wanted all those weeks ago, when he had first learned of Della's death. Now, though, looking at Dora's distraught face, it felt like a Pyrrhic victory. She looked so small and alone.

'That's not going to happen. Archie needs you.'

'No, he needs his mum.' Her grey eyes were

clouded with pain. 'But he can't have her, so he needs the next best thing—and that's not me. Even Della thought that.'

'Of course she didn't. She just didn't—'

'Didn't what? Have time to put it in her will?' She gave a short, brittle laugh. 'You didn't know her. She made time for everything. She was waiting to see if I could change, become a better person. But I didn't—*I haven't*. I couldn't even sing "Happy Birthday".'

The bruise in her voice made something rip inside him. When she hadn't started singing he'd thought at first that she was waiting for him to give her a signal. But then he had looked at her face and seen the fear. No shock or confusion, though, and that meant it had happened before.

Brain racing, he thought back to that video of her, the breathtaking luminosity of her talent. How had it happened? The sudden silencing of that voice?

'Is that why you stopped singing? Did it happen before?'

She nodded. 'So, you see, I didn't put Archie first.' Her eyes met his, daring him to disagree. 'I'm not noble or selfless. I stopped because I couldn't sing.'

'And this happened when?'

He knew he'd sounded harsh, but her confession angered him. Why was she dealing with this alone?

'I don't know. Maybe a month after Della died. What does it matter? I wanted to sing for Della. I was going to sing her favourite song, but I couldn't.'

She was crying again, and he felt a pain he had never experienced before rise in his throat—a pain so bad he thought he might choke. And then he stopped thinking and pulled her into his arms again. Only this time he wasn't going to let her go.

'You were still in shock, grieving. Whoever let you on a stage should be shot.' He felt her hands ball against his chest, heard her sob.

'I can't make it make sense…her going like that…'

'It's okay. I've got you.'

He held her close, letting her cry, stroking her hair and speaking softly until finally he felt the stiffness in her body ease.

'You have a beautiful voice, Dora,' he said gently.

'Not any more.' She sniffed. 'And I don't mind. I deserve it. I made her life so difficult.'

The flatness in her voice made his breathing jam. 'No…'

'It's true. She was so upset when I dropped out of uni. But I dropped out because I'd been offered a recording contract. I wanted to surprise her—only I never got the chance.'

'I'm so sorry,' he said quietly.

Tears were streaking her cheeks. 'They were nice about it, but I couldn't sing, so…' She turned away from him. 'I should have told you this before, then you wouldn't have asked me to sing, and I wouldn't have let you down in front of your family.'

'Shh…nobody noticed, I promise. We were all too busy trying to stay in tune.' He smoothed his thumbs over her cheeks. 'And if anyone was let down it was you. By me. I didn't think about what today would be like for you without Della. I didn't make you feel you could tell me. But I want that to change. From now on, I want us to be honest.'

She breathed out shakily. 'You know, you're much nicer now than when we first met.'

He smiled. 'I'm keeping better company now.'

Her mouth quivered. 'I didn't mean what I said…about Archie.'

'I know.' He cupped her face in his hands. 'I

know how much you love him—and he loves you. I'd call that a Royal Flush.'

Her grey eyes lifted to his. 'No, it's a straight flush. Having you as a brother and being part of your wonderful family makes it a Royal Flush.'

He nodded, barely missing a beat. Honesty in this instance served no purpose. His sisters' acceptance meant a lot to Dora, and after everything she had just told him he wasn't about to take that away from her.

But he couldn't look her in the eye and lie. Instead, he lowered his mouth to hers and kissed her.

Her lips parted and he deepened the kiss, losing himself in the softness of her mouth and the silken feel of her hair. This wasn't a lie. His desire for her was real and honest. And wasn't that what they had agreed?

Here in bed he could give himself to her unconditionally. Here, with Dora, he could forget he was a Lao, forget the expectations and pretence his name demanded. He was just a man. And this was just sex.

Breaking the kiss, he shifted away from her. Slowly, gently, his eyes watching her for any signs that she wanted him to stop, he reached round and unzipped her dress. He slid it down over her body, his breath catching as he saw that she wasn't wearing a bra. Cupping her breasts in his hands, he felt her skin quiver. The nipples were already standing proud and taut, and his eyes still on hers, her ran his thumbs over them, his pulse accelerating as she breathed out unsteadily.

'You have no idea how much I need you right now,' he said softly.

'I need you too,' she whispered and, taking his hand, pressed it against the damp heat between her thighs.

This time they took it slowly. This time they were two people who could take their time. Now nothing was forbidden.

His skin was humming with need, his blood pounding in his groin like the waves crashing against the cliffs that edged his estate.

Pushing her back gently against the bed, he drew her panties down her legs. She was naked now, and he gazed down at her dry-mouthed, a pulse beating in his throat, his eyes roaming hungrily over her breasts and stomach and down to the triangle of dark blonde curls.

Her eyes were dark and glazed and, leaning forward, he kissed her softly. 'You're so beautiful, Dora.' He brushed his lips over hers, feeling them part, and then he slid down the bed and put his hands between her thighs, spreading them apart.

She lifted her hips a little, helping him, and, lowering his head, he put his tongue on her. Her body tensed, arching upwards, and her fingers tightened in his hair as he flattened his tongue against her core, feeling her pulse beat against him, her soft moan making his body shake with a passion he had never felt before.

Satisfying his lovers had always mattered to him, but this was different. Dora's pleasure was not just important to him—it was entwined with his.

'Now. Please. I need you now.'

She was pushing against him, her hands grabbing at his shoulders, guiding him up the bed as though he was blind.

He resisted for a moment, and then he let himself be led, leaning over her, licking her breast, her shoulder, kissing her neck, her collarbone, his mouth seeking hers as he pushed into her.

Her legs locked over his thighs, anchoring him against her, and he began to move slowly, curbing his need to fill her body with the heat and hunger that was stretching his body to its limits, not wanting it to end.

She was panting now, her breath hot and urgent. He felt her arch beneath him, and then her hands were clutching his shoulders and her muscles were clenching around him with such force that he couldn't hold back another second. Groaning, he thrust inside her a final time.

CHAPTER EIGHT

CHARLIE FELT HIS muscles coil sharply, like a snake. Dancing to the left, he ducked his head, breathing in sharply as Mario's glove caught him on the chest. He was getting tired now, eating punches, and he changed direction, trying to relax his core, circling around to his trainer's left side, his right glove close to his face.

And then, just like that, it was over.

He bumped fists with Mario and, breathing out, pulled off his gloves and slipped out his mouthguard.

Working out was part of his daily routine, and to avoid him getting bored with the usual mix of HIIT Mario had introduced boxing into their sessions. Mostly they just trained together, working with the pads or the bag, but this morning Charlie had wanted to spar, hoping that the impact of Mario's blows would somehow displace the pain in his chest—Dora's pain.

Stepping under the rainfall shower, he closed

his eyes, his skin tensing as cold water hit his body like hundreds of freezing needles. Turning slowly beneath the powerful spray, he tilted his face upwards.

He had woken early to find his arm around Dora's waist, her soft body spooning his, one hand tucked beneath her cheek, the other palm flat against the sheet. In sleep she looked younger—absurdly young.

His mouth twisted. Much too young to be entering into a marriage of convenience. She deserved better. She needed TLC.

Yes, he could make her life comfortable. Give her security, an allowance, nice dresses. But he hadn't signed on for her secrets and her pain.

And yet he couldn't stop thinking about what she had told him. Or the way she had told him—as if it was spilling out of her. A part of him wanted to tell her that he understood her pain only too clearly, but the more she told him, the less he could tell her.

He didn't want to add to her pain with his. Even though he had told her that he wanted to be honest, he couldn't burden her with that.

Smoothing the water from his face, he breathed out. Her distress after the party had been so real, so sharp, he could still feel the puncture wounds around his heart.

And pressing up against his heart, filling the space like a dark cloud, was guilt.

Stepping out of the shower, he took a towel and began to dry himself.

Everything he had thought about the woman lying in his bed was wrong. She wasn't some university dropout with no direction, or a party girl using her job as a casino waitress to target sugar daddies.

She was just a young woman who had been dealt a two-seven—the worst hand in poker.

Abandoned by her mother, unwanted and ignored by her father, she had now lost the one person in her life who'd loved her, and that had led to her losing her voice and a career.

And then, when she had still been grieving and broken, he had come along and tried to take Archie.

It sickened him that he had done that—that he had considered it acceptable, normal, to behave with such casual ruthlessness.

When had he become that man?

Why had he become that man?

But he knew why.

It had been the only way to stay within the

orbit of his father's love. Outside of that orbit there had been nothing but a cold, endless dark. And he had seen what it was like not to matter to Lao Dan—to be pushed out into the darkness that had swallowed up his mother. And that had scared him. So he had been willing—eager, in fact, to do whatever had been necessary to earn his father's approval.

Whatever had been necessary.

It was easy to say. It had always been easy to do. But now what mattered was doing what was right.

For Archie's sake, Dora needed to know that Della had not just loved her, but trusted her.

He wanted to do that for her. In fact he wanted to do more than that. He wanted to make her believe in herself again, so that one day she would be able to sing as she had in those videos.

'Here you are.'

Leaning forward, Dora handed Archie another soft ball, and watched as he stuffed it into the open mouth of a cheery-looking orange monster which promptly spat it out.

She laughed as he gave a squeal of delight. It had been one of his birthday presents from Charlie's sisters and he absolutely loved it.

'Hi. Mind if I come in? I just want to run something by you.'

Glancing up, she felt her heart flip over. Charlie was standing in the doorway, holding a large white envelope in one hand. His hair was damp and sleek from the shower and, as usual, her brain was unreasonably distracted by his dark eyes and the curve of his cheekbones.

It was the first time she had seen him since last night. Since they had made love again and she had cried all over him. *Again.*

It had been so embarrassing. He must think so too—otherwise why was he suddenly being so formal, standing in the doorway asking for permission to enter?

Maybe if she just acted as if none of it had happened…

But then she thought back to what he had said yesterday, about being honest with each other. Glancing over to where Archie was now enthusiastically hugging the monster, she felt a trickle of hope dilute her panic.

The fact was that, without planning to do so, she had already been honest with Charlie and the sky hadn't fallen on her head. He already knew everything—good and bad. Either she had told him or he had known it already from that dumb report.

And if there was one truth that was truer than all the rest, it was that she wanted to give Archie a good life. And for that to happen she needed the two of them to work.

She took a breath. 'Okay, but first I just want to say sorry for what happened yesterday. I don't know why I keep crying all over you. I mean, I know why I'm upset, it's just that's not how I normally behave.'

Her heartbeat stumbled. She had a well-practised strategy for dealing with pain and sadness. Basically, she just pushed anything bad out of her head and it worked out fine.

Of course Della hadn't ever been fooled, but the rest of the world had never suspected that she was hurting inside—or how much.

Only for some reason, with Charlie, she seemed to turn into a sobbing wreck.

Unwilling to probe as to why that should be the case, she gave him a quick, careful smile. 'Anyway, I just wanted to say sorry.'

He frowned. 'There's no need to apologise.' Pushing away from the door, he walked over and sat down beside her. 'Yesterday was always going to be a hard day,' he said quietly.

Something in his tone made her breathing slow and, looking across at him, she felt a swell of guilt rise up inside her like the wash from a boat.

For her, Archie's birthday celebrations had been tinged with sadness because Della was missing. But for the first time it occurred to her that there was someone else who should have been at the party but hadn't.

Lao Dan.

Her stomach knotted. Up until now she had only thought about him briefly, and mainly in relation to that fact that Archie no longer had a father.

But Charlie had lost a father too.

'Yes, it was.' She hesitated, and then, reaching out, touched him lightly on the arm. 'It must have been hard for you and your sisters, not having your dad there, and I didn't think about that.'

He shook his head. 'It's not the same, Dora. My father was an old man. He had lived a good life—the life he wanted. It made sense, him dying—not like Della.'

She bit her lip. 'But you must miss him so much.'

How could he not? Charlie was running his father's business; there must be reminders everywhere, every day, just like there was for her with Della.

For a moment he didn't answer, and then his hand found hers.

'He always liked getting the family together. It was important to him. But I'm not sure that having a party was such a good idea for you.'

He looked tense, unhappy, and she felt something inside her pinch.

'But it was.' Her fingers tightened around his. 'Archie loved every minute of it. And I know I got upset, but I really did enjoy it—especially meeting your sisters. They were so kind to me, and so friendly.'

She felt the muscles in her face stiffen. At the time she had been relieved and grateful that everyone had so readily accepted the news of their engagement. Now, though, she felt ashamed and guilty.

His sisters couldn't possibly want their brother to marry a cocktail waitress he had known for less than a fortnight. But they had acted as if they were perfectly happy with the news. Not just out of politeness, but out of love. They loved their brother, and they thought that she and Charlie were in love.

Only how would they feel about her if they knew the truth?

'What is it?' he asked.

Looking up at him, she pulled a face. 'They think we're in love. It feels wrong. Lying to them. I know that's what we're going to have to do, but it's hard—and I think it's going to be harder for you. I don't have anyone. But you're going to have to pretend to your whole family that we're in love.' She hesitated. 'And then there's your mother...'

Nuria. Lao Dan's widow.

She knew he had told his mother they were engaged, but she had no idea how she had reacted to the news that her son was marrying the sister of her husband's mistress.

Her throat tightened. She could make a pretty educated guess.

He didn't reply, just stared past her.

Trying to fill the silence, she began speaking in a rush. 'I just know that if Della was here I couldn't lie to her. I wouldn't be able to—I wouldn't want to. And I don't want you to have—'

'It's fine, Dora.'

Curving his arm around her waist, he pulled her onto his lap, and she had a sudden fierce flashback to that first, feverish time they had made love in the library.

'Everything's going to be fine.' His dark eyes held hers. 'You just need to focus on what is true. That, together, we've found a way to make this work for Archie.'

That was easy for him to say. He could make anything work. He was the CEO of a hotel casino empire. His entire life ran like one those expensive Swiss watches with all the cogs and dials. She doubted he had ever messed up anything.

Whereas she had never finished anything she'd started.

'Dora, look at me.'

Reluctantly, she looked up.

'I could tell you that you are an amazing young woman, and that you have been braver and stronger than anyone I've ever met. And I could tell you that Archie is lucky to have you. But I don't think you'd believe me.'

Capturing her chin, he tilted her face so that there was nowhere to look but into his eyes.

'And I get that. I haven't made it easy for you to trust me. I don't think anyone ever has except Della. That's why I want you to have these.'

He held up the envelope and she stared at it uncertainly. 'What's that?'

'It's the letters Della wrote to my father.'

She stared at the envelope, breathing out against the sudden sharp ache in her heart. 'Have you read them?'

Of course he hadn't, she thought a half-second later as he shook his head. His mother had been married to Lao Dan when he died. Why would Charlie want to read love letters from his father's mistress?

'He showed me a couple. After he had the first stroke.' He glanced over at Archie. 'I'll take him somewhere and you can read them.'

'No—stay. Please. I'd rather you stayed,' she said quietly and, taking the envelope, tipped out the letters.

Most were handwritten, and that felt odd, seeing her sister's familiar cursive writing. But more strange still was meeting this version of Della.

Dora had always been the one talking and telling stories, teasing and trying to get Della to be more impulsive. Her sister had always been contained, measured, sensible.

Not this Della, though: she had been provocative and passionate.

A lot like me, Dora thought. And that was a surprise too.

Reading her sister's words, she felt sadness

and joy alternately filling her chest. It was heart-breaking to know that Della's happiness had been so short-lived, but her excitement at finding love for the first time shone from the page.

Dora's heartbeat froze.

Her name jumped out at her from the pages of closely scrawled writing.

I can't wait for you to meet Dora. She's so talented. She could have anything she wants—not that she believes me.

And there it was again.

Dora is really excited about our news. Our baby is going to be so lucky to have her in his life.

There was more, but she couldn't read it. Her eyes were too full of tears to see.

'Do-Do.'

Archie was beside her, his dark eyes huge, his forehead creasing with confusion, and she pulled him into her arms, burying her face in his neck, breathing in his baby smell as he patted her clumsily on the shoulder.

Finally, she lifted her head. Charlie was watching her in silence. She held out the letters, but he shook his head.

'Keep them. She would have wanted you to have them. I want you to have them.'

'She never talked to me about their relationship.' She bit her lip. 'Probably because I just used to get angry and say horrible things about him.'

'He hurt her,' he said simply. 'Of course you were angry. I was angry too. With Della. She always seemed so straightforward. I thought I knew her, and I trusted her. Only then...'

'She hurt you?'

He nodded. 'But she was good for him. She made him a better person. A nicer person...'

He paused, and she could see he was struggling to form a sentence.

'You've been honest with me, and I want to be honest with you. I think my father would have left my mother to be with her, but I talked him out of it. I made him choose my mother and me over Della and Archie.'

Dora breathed out unsteadily, shocked by his words. So Lao Dan had loved Della.

For a moment she thought back to her sister's sadness, and the heartache that had coloured the last year of her life. It could have been so different…

But would she have felt any differently, acted any differently, if she had been in Charlie's position?

'I don't think you made him choose,' she said slowly. 'Your father doesn't sound to me like the kind of man who would have had his mind changed by anyone. I think you probably just gave him permission to do what he wanted.'

He stared at her in silence. 'I didn't think about Della or Archie.'

'Della was a grown-up.' Her eyes met his. 'She knew your father was married before she became his mistress and she made a choice. Maybe it didn't work out how she wanted, but she didn't have any regrets.'

Except one. Just once, after Lao Dan's death, Della had admitted wishing she had done more to fight for him—whatever the outcome.

She cleared her throat. 'And you love Archie now, but he wasn't real to you then—any more than your dad was ever real to me.'

Clearly he felt guilty for making his father choose. That was why he had been so determined to get Archie back.

'Now, everything you're doing is for him.'

Something squeezed around her heart. Even marrying a woman he didn't love. 'You're putting him first.'

'So are you,' he said, pulling her closer so that Archie was between the two of them. 'That's why we're getting married.'

Breathing out, she leaned into him. It was why they were getting married, but for some reason she wished it wasn't.

'Yes, it is.' She managed to smile up at him.

'So let's spend today together as a family,' he said. He stared down at her, his dark eyes fixed on hers. 'And then, this evening, you and I are going out. Just the two of us.'

'Out?'

'Now that we've told my family, I want to show off my fiancée to the world.'

She gazed at him, trying to evaluate his words, wondering what it would feel like if he meant what he said. But to think that way was pointless. She couldn't bring herself to submit to that kind of vulnerability—particularly when Charlie couldn't have made it any clearer that Archie was the reason they were marrying.

It was already dark by the time the limousine left the house for the Black Tiger that evening. But no amount of darkness could extinguish Dora's luminous beauty, Charlie thought, gazing over at the woman sitting on his left.

Her blonde hair was loose and, reaching out, he caught a strand between his fingers. Turning, she looked up at him, her mouth softening into a smile and he felt his groin harden.

'You look beautiful.'

More than beautiful. She was making his teeth ache.

His eyes travelled appreciatively over her body. She was wearing a silver dress that clung to her skin exactly where he wanted to touch her most.

It was only the presence of his driver and the bodyguard in the front of the car that was stopping him from pulling her onto his lap and letting his hands roam at will over all the curves and lines of her.

'Thank you—you look pretty good yourself,' she said softly. 'So, where are you taking me?'

'To the Black Tiger. I thought you might like to try your luck on the tables.'

She laughed. 'That's going to be complicated—awkward, even. I mean, if I win big, you lose.'

A pulse beat across his skin. 'You're going to be my wife; I win big either way.'

For a moment their eyes locked, and then, leaning forward, she kissed him lightly on the mouth. 'You're nice, you know...'

He thought her voice sounded shaky, almost sad. But then she deepened the kiss, pulling him closer so that he could feel the heat of her body through her dress, and he stopped thinking completely...

She did win at roulette—and then lost it all on the blackjack table.

Afterwards they went to the famous Black Bar, to sample the legendary Tiger Martinis.

'Wow!' she said as she took a sip. 'What's in it?'

'I don't know the exact recipe. Orson—' he nodded over at the barman '—keeps that a closely guarded secret. But basically it's some kind of chocolate liqueur and *baijiu* instead of vodka. Do you like it?'

'I do. It's delicious.' Her grey eyes were dancing beneath the soft lighting. 'So, does someone actually play that? Or is it just for show?'

Her words snagged on something in his head, and it took a moment for him to follow her gaze towards the gleaming black Steinway piano.

'Oh, it gets played. In fact, I think the show's about to start.'

A young male pianist ran through a programme

of popular songs, but Charlie barely registered the familiar tunes. He was too busy watching Dora.

She was beautiful, but before her beauty had been a distraction that had dazzled and frustrated him. He had wanted her, and it had angered him that she had the power to reduce him to being just a man. Now, though, he could see past the soft mouth and the delicate jaw. He could see that even when she was smiling there was a lost quality to her—as if she had strayed off the path and was trying to pretend to herself, and to everyone around her, that she knew her way home.

It made his stomach hurt, thinking about it, and, picking up his glass, he finished his drink as a scattered round of applause signalled the end of the pianist's set.

'What do you think?' he said quietly.

She turned, smiling. 'He's very good.'

He held her gaze. 'I thought we were going to be honest with one another?'

Her beautiful pink mouth curved up at the corners. 'Okay, then, honestly? He's adequate. He's a competent pianist, but he's lazy. To me it feels like he's hiding behind the melodies. But, to be fair, it's hard to pull out a good performance every time.'

Remembering the videos he'd watched, he shook his head. 'You did.'

She gave him a small, twisted smile. 'I was unhappy. Inside, I felt like everything was going to fly apart. Singing was pretty much the only time I felt solid and whole.'

'And you think that's what it takes to be a good performer? Unhappiness?'

'No,' she said slowly. 'But I think you have to *need* to perform. I don't mean for money. It has to feed something inside.' She screwed up her face. 'I'm not explaining it very well, but you can feel when it's there. It's like you can't look away.'

Exactly. That was how he had felt, watching those videos of her. How he felt now. But of course this was a performance too, he thought, ignoring how that made the knot in his stomach tighten.

'You explain it very well. So well that I'd like to offer you a job. How would you like to oversee the entertainment side of things here for me?'

She stared at his face. 'Won't the person currently overseeing it mind?'

'There is no one. But I clearly need someone—and you obviously have what it takes.'

'Are you being serious?'

He nodded. 'It's an area I've been looking to

improve for some time now. I just needed the right person. And now I've found her.'

'Okay, well... I could think about it.'

The eagerness she was trying to hide made him suddenly regret his offer.

Tonight had been meant to make a statement. *This is my world. This is my wife.* And it should have been easy, bringing the two together. Surely that was why it was called a marriage of convenience?

Only it didn't feel convenient—it felt confusing.

Living as a Lao might offer a life of insane luxury, but only the strong survived—and he and his sisters all bore the scars of endless competition. How could he lead Dora and Archie into that arena?

But if he didn't, he might lose both of them.

'Are you okay?'

Dora was looking at him, her face flushed with excitement, and suddenly he wanted to leave. To go where it would be just the two of them, as he'd promised her.

'I'm fine.' He squeezed her hand, walling off the confusion in his head. 'Are you hungry?'

She nodded.

'Then let's get out of here.'

'Where are we going?' she asked a moment later, as they walked out of the hotel and down to a private jetty that jutted out into the bay.

Ignoring the bodyguards, he turned towards her and pulled her against him. A current was running through him of heat and hope and fear, and he needed to contain it, to get back control.

'I'm tired of people. I want it to be just the two of us.'

'I thought you wanted to show me the city?'

'I do. I will,' he said softly, and he led her towards the shimmering dark water and the beautiful boat moored at the end of the jetty.

'Oh, my goodness!'

Charlie gazed over to where she was looking, trying to see it through her eyes.

Made of ironwood and teak, and built by hand on the Pearl River Delta, the junk was ludicrous, beautiful, pointless, indulgent. But he loved it.

Out on the water he was answerable to no one. And he loved sailing at night. It felt good, pushing back against the darkness that was always lurking at the edges of his life.

Dora bit into the smile curving her mouth. 'It looks like a pirate ship.'

He glanced up at the blood-red batwing sails.

'In that case, maybe I should take you prisoner,' he said softly.

She had slipped off her shoes, and she looked so beautiful and sexy, standing in her bare feet, that before he knew what he was doing he had scooped her up in his arms.

'And what if I try and escape? Will you make me walk the plank?'

He shook his head. 'Only as a last resort. But first...' He paused and, watching her eyes darken, felt his body respond hungrily.

'But first what?' she said hoarsely.

'First I'd try and think of something that might persuade you to stay.' He searched her face. 'Can you think of anything?'

He heard her swallow.

'Yes...' she murmured and, reaching up, clasped his face in her hands and kissed him frantically. 'Yes.'

He carried her below deck, kicking open the door to the cabin and dropping her onto the bed.

She was pulling at his clothes, fingers fumbling with his tie, his buttons. 'Help me,' she whispered. Reaching up, she clasped his face, kissing him urgently.

His heart was slamming against his ribs like a door in a high wind. He yanked at his clothes, his erection straining against his trousers as she tugged his shirt free of his waistband, then worked his belt through the buckle.

His hand caught in her hair and he sucked in a breath as she pulled him free. He felt her fingers wrap around his hard length as she drew him closer, and then his whole body tensed as she dipped her mouth forward, flicking her tongue over the smooth, taut head.

He breathed out shakily as she shifted backwards, her eyes dark and hazy, and, reaching out, pulled her to her feet.

'Take it off,' he said softly.

He watched, the blood pounding round his body, as she slipped her thin straps off her shoulders and the dress slid over her body, pooling at her feet. She stared at him in silence, and then she pushed her panties down too.

He had been going to take it slowly, but now, gazing at her body, he felt his muscles tighten with the need to be inside her.

She must be thinking the same thing too. Reaching out, she pulled him towards her, her mouth finding his, her nipples brushing against the bare skin of his chest.

His hands captured her waist and, pressing her against him, he kissed her fiercely. She was kissing him back, and his whole body stiffened as he felt her fingers start to stroke the thick length of his erection.

It was too much.

Grunting, he caught her hand. 'Turn around,' he said hoarsely.

His breath caught in his throat as he slid his arm around her waist, lifting her onto the bed so that she was on her knees. He found her throat, kissing the smooth skin, pressing his body against the smooth curve of her bottom, and then he gripped her hips and pushed into her, began to move.

His hand captured her breast, squeezing the nipple, and then he reached down and ran his thumb over the swollen bud, his body hardening at the soft moaning noise she was making.

'Yes…yes…'

She was panting, her hips working in time with his, and their bodies were slick with sweat as, with an arch of her back, he felt her come.

Body shuddering, she cried out. And then she batted his hand away and he felt her hand cupping him. He was jerking against her, his grunt of pleasure mingling with her ragged breathing as he spilled inside her with hot, liquid force.

* * *

Neither of them wanted to leave the cabin, so he had a meal brought to them, and they sat up in bed, eating with their fingers.

They made love again, more slowly this time, and then Dora fell asleep in his arms.

He breathed out slowly.

He was calmer now.

Here on the boat it worked—they worked.

She shifted beside him in her sleep and he gazed down at her, feeling his muscles clench.

It wasn't just the sex.

Earlier at the casino he'd felt on edge, and it had been the same at Archie's party. Each time it had been the same—that same feeling of being pulled in two directions. But why?

He thought back to what Dora had said earlier. How she hated the idea of lying to his sisters, and in particular having to lie about them being in love.

But she didn't understand how his family worked.

His sisters knew his father had asked him to do whatever was necessary to bring Archie to Macau. And so, even though they didn't believe in his engagement at all, they had gone along with it—because maintaining the myth of 'family' took priority over everything.

They knew the score. Or they thought they did.

His heart began hammering inside his chest.

Dora had been worried, thinking it would be hard for him having to pretend that he was in love with her. His sisters had known he was simply following his father's strict mantra of family first.

And maybe it had been like that at first, but now...

He felt something like panic, confusion, and then denial. This couldn't be happening to him. His life was planned, and he hadn't planned on feeling anything for Dora.

Only the truth was...he wasn't pretending to be in love.

His heart was beating wildly.

It wasn't true. It couldn't be true.

He searched inside himself, but every turn he made inside his head led him back to the same place.

He loved her. He loved Dora.

Part of him wanted to wake her and tell her—but what was he expecting her to say?

He had cornered her, coaxed her and nudged

her into agreeing to this marriage for Archie's sake. He'd offered sex and security.

Love hadn't been mentioned.

And, however much it might hurt to say nothing, he knew he couldn't mention it now.

CHAPTER NINE

DORA WOKE AT DAWN.

The sun was still low, just a soft veil of light, but it was enough to pull her from the cocoon of sleep and make her eyelids flutter open.

Charlie's arm was resting on her thigh, the heat from his body seeping into her skin, and for a moment she let herself enjoy the weight and warmth of it, the pictures it made in her head.

She wanted to believe in those pictures—wanted them to be real.

Her eyes rested on his face. A lock of dark hair had fallen across his forehead and she had to clench her hands to stop herself from reaching to smooth it away.

No wonder she had let her thoughts stray into the dangerous territory of what it would feel like if this was real. If they were really in love. He was so beautiful, sexy and smart, and unbelievably good in bed.

But it was just like in the movies.

Two people had to want to walk into the sunset. And for Charlie the sunset was nothing more than a giant distant star sinking beneath the horizon. It held no magic or romance—or at least not with her.

And, to be fair, he had never so much as hinted that it did. He had been honest about his motives for inviting her to Macau, and for asking her to marry him.

Archie was his sole concern.

Hers too.

Love—the walking into the sunset kind anyway—was beyond her. Della might have thought Dora just needed to meet the 'right' man, but she knew she wasn't brave enough to risk having the stuffing ripped out of her.

She was just confused. So many things had happened in such a short time in the blur of her new life. Della's accident, becoming Archie's guardian, meeting Charlie...

And then there was the past, always tripping her up, making her want things she knew she couldn't let herself have even if they were on offer.

Her chest tightened, so that she felt suddenly breathless, trapped.

Lifting Charlie's arm, she slid across the bed and sat up.

It took a few moments for her to make sense of the cabin, and then, picking up the shirt he'd discarded so hastily last night, she shrugged it on and crept from the room.

There was nobody about on deck, and she walked towards the front of the boat. After the warmth of the cabin it was refreshingly cool and, leaning against the handrail, she gazed across the water, breathing in deeply.

The sun was inching higher, its light getting brighter, shifting from white to yellow. But on the mainland the hotels and casinos were still lit up, the flickering reds and greens and pinks drawing people in with promises of winning big.

Wrapping her arms around her waist, she hugged herself tightly.

Charlie was like those pulsing lights. He had lured her in, pulling her close, and part of her had wanted to be pulled closer. Closeness was what she craved more than anything.

It was an age-old longing.

A wistful yearning for someone to look inside her and like what they saw.

Always before she had found the hope of it too weighty even to think about. Instead it had been easier to end things quickly and start from scratch again.

But things with Charlie had moved so fast there had been no time to blink. And it didn't help losing the one person who had held all the broken pieces of her together.

That was why she was feeling like this now. She was just looking to fill the empty space, letting her desire to be loved override common sense.

So what if Charlie had held her while she cried? Or bought her dresses? Or even offered her a job? He was a good man.

In a lot of ways he was like her sister. He took responsibility for things, for people. Look at how he had stepped up for his family after his father's death. And, like he said, she was part of that family now.

Probably that too was a reason for why she was feeling like this. Even when their father had still been living with them they had really never been a family. They had shared the same house, but he had been autonomous, orbiting his daughters and only interacting with them when necessary.

Della had been both sister and mother to her, so to suddenly find herself invited into this ready-made dynastic family was mind-blowing for Dora. And it was the blur of these new and sudden changes to her life that was making her feel things, good and bad, that she wasn't used to feeling, that she had never allowed herself to feel.

But she would get used to it—to all of it—and then, when she was more in control of everything, she would be fine.

Looking up at the fluttering red sails, she sighed.

It was being on this damned boat...it was just so stupidly romantic.

'Hey.'

She turned her head, her heart jumping. Blinking in the daylight, Charlie was standing on the deck, his dark hair tousled, the top button of his trousers unbuttoned so that the waistband hung low, revealing the toned muscles of his stomach.

'Hey, yourself,' she said, holding herself perfectly still.

He looked too beautiful, too impossibly sexy to be real, and that he should be here with her felt so improbable that she was suddenly scared to move in case he might disappear like a mirage.

She watched as he walked slowly towards her, not bothering to hide the hunger she knew was showing on her face. Desire was good. Desire was allowed. Both of them had agreed to that, and she could see her own desire mirrored in his dark gaze.

He stopped in front of her, his eyes drifting down over her body in a way that made her stomach start to clench and unclench.

'I borrowed your shirt. You don't mind, do you?'

'Not at all. It looks a lot better on you than me.'

That was debatable, she thought. But before she could reply he caught her arm and pulled her against him, forking his fingers through her hair and capturing her mouth softly with his. The gentleness of his kiss made her lean into the warmth of his body.

Lifting his head, he breathed out unsteadily. 'Why didn't you wake me?'

She shrugged. 'I didn't want to. You looked so sweet.'

He grimaced. 'Babies are sweet. And puppies.'

Pressing her hands against the smooth contours of his chest, she smiled. 'Well, we agreed to be honest with one another—and, *honestly*, you looked sweet.'

His arm tightened around her waist. 'You do know it's a good hour to swim back to shore from here?'

Tilting her head to the side, she stared up at

him. 'You pirates are all the same—so thin-skinned and image-conscious.'

'Know a lot of pirates, do you?'

She felt his hand flex against her skin. 'None, actually.' She gave a faint smile. 'In fact, Della used to say I always picked pushovers.'

He raised an eyebrow. 'I've never been called a pushover before.'

'You don't count.'

His eyes narrowed. 'This conversation is doing wonders for my ego.'

Bursting out laughing, she pushed his arm lightly, her heart beating wildly as his mouth curved up into one of those rare, irresistible smiles.

'I mean, I didn't pick you. We didn't pick each other. Archie did.'

'Yes, I suppose that's true.'

Something stirred beneath the surface of his face and he started to speak again, then stopped.

In the silence that followed he stared past her, his gaze following a pair of gulls as they swooped low over the water and then up towards the sun. She watched him swallow, watched a muscle tighten in his jaw.

It was as if her pulse was suddenly marking time. There was no reason why she should be holding her breath, no explanation for why every nerve in her body seemed to be drawn tight, but all at once nothing seemed as important as what he was going to say next.

'What we spoke about last night—did you mean it? About helping with the entertainment side of the casino?'

She stared at him in confusion.

Was that it?

The change of subject away from the personal to the professional was entirely unexpected and, thrown off balance, she shook her head, then nodded. 'Yes, I meant it.'

Her stomach clenched. Suddenly it was what she wanted more than anything. One day she might find her voice again, but this was something she could do—something she would enjoy doing.

'Have you changed your mind?' she asked.

He shook his head, his eyes resting on hers. 'I need someone who understands that area of the business…someone I can trust.' The tension in his jaw had eased, softening his voice. 'And I'd like that someone to be you.'

A rush of warmth lifted her slightly off her feet. It was something she hadn't felt in a long time, and then only infrequently. It was a feeling of mattering, of having something to say that made a difference to people, and it had only happened when she was on stage.

Not even Della had made her feel this way.

Her sister had been so much older, so composed. It had always been hard to feel like her equal. And yet, despite the glaring discrepancy between their wealth, for some reason—probably the fact that they were co-parenting Archie—she did feel like Charlie's equal.

'I'd like that too.'

'My beautiful, talented wife,' he said softly. He was staring at her steadily. 'Everyone is going to go crazy for you at the engagement party.'

Engagement party. What engagement party?

Catching sight of her expression, he made a face. 'Sorry, I meant to tell you last night, but it slipped my mind.'

She felt her cheeks grow hot and the skin tighten over her bones, remembering how he had turned her around, the weight and the firmness of his body against hers and the smooth, hard tension of his skin.

There had been no conscious thought in that cabin. Or boundaries. Their hunger for one another had blotted out reason and self-control.

'I'm not surprised,' she said softly.

His eyes gleamed and, catching her chin, he tilted her face up to his. 'I hope you don't mind. My sisters are planning it. It's kind of their thing.'

Her throat felt too tight to speak. They had told his family, and last night at the casino she had been by his side as his fiancée. But an engagement party made everything official, public, high-profile. The Lao family was big news in the Eastern hemisphere—the engagement of Lao Dan's eldest son would not go unnoticed by the media.

Or by his mother, she thought, her heart lurching drunkenly against her ribs.

It went without saying that Nuria would be invited. Under any other circumstances she would have met his mother already. But there was one blindingly obvious reason why that hadn't happened.

She was Della's sister, and it didn't take much imagination to guess at what Nuria must be feeling right now. Or why Charlie was not rushing to introduce the two of them to one another.

She felt her heart start to pound.

No mother would want her son to marry the sister of her husband's mistress. But surely Nuria would have to go—*would want to go*—to her son's engagement party.

For a moment she thought about asking him, but the thought of introducing something that might jeopardise this easy intimacy between them made her courage fail, and instead she said quickly, 'No, of course not. I think it's a lovely idea. Is there anything I can do to help?'

'I don't know. I could ask them.' He seemed surprised, and then he leaned in closer, the corners of his mouth curving slightly. 'Actually, there is one thing. Do you think maybe you could help them choose the entertainment?'

'You mean you want to see if I've got what it takes before you let me loose on your casino?'

His dark eyes locked on hers and slowly he unbuttoned the front of the shirt. She felt cool air, and then the warm palm of his hand on her skin. It was suddenly difficult to find a breath.

'I've seen everything I need to see, and you've definitely got what it takes.'

He was talking about her body, about sex—and yet he wasn't. Her heart began to pound. Proposing, getting married...that was for Archie. But this was different—a part of it, but separate.

He could have turned down her offer of help, fobbed her off, but he hadn't. Just as he hadn't needed to ask her to help with overseeing the entertainment at the casino.

Her pulse was racing; she felt dizzy. Suddenly her heart felt too busy for her chest.

He wanted her in his life.

Wanted her for her.

The dizziness faded abruptly.

No, that wasn't true. She just wanted it to be true in the same way she wanted to believe that when he held her close it was more than just sex.

She tried telling herself again that she was just confused—tried really hard to shake off the feeling, to push it away. But it had been building like a wave at sea, and now nothing—no logic, no amount of denial—could stop it from crashing over her.

Just like nothing had stopped her from falling in love with him.

Winded by the truth, she stared at him dazedly as he touched her face, brushing his thumb over her bottom lip.

'You'd be doing us all a favour, Dora. Like I said before, none of them can hold a note—and besides, their musical taste is a little…how can I put it?…*vanilla.*'

She managed to smile, but inside she was running. Running from the hope and the despair filling her heart.

How had she let this happen?

For so long she had managed to look the other way, and even though there had been moments when she had felt herself turning she had convinced herself that it was just the same longing to belong. That it was just her body watching him, reaching out to him, waiting for him.

But all the time her heart had been following the magnetic pull of his north, drawn not by loneliness but by love.

She managed to smile. 'I can see that would be a problem for you. I mean, vanilla's not really your thing, is it?'

'Not with you,' he said softly.

He smoothed the skin of her cheek, his dark eyes intent on hers. 'There's something else. Saturday is Qingming. It's a lot like the Day of the Dead. We visit our ancestors' graves and pay our respects. It's an important day—the whole family will be there.'

The whole family.

Her heart began beating out of time. 'You mean me and Archie too?'

He nodded. 'I know it's a lot to ask, but I would like you both to come with me.'

'And that would be okay, would it? With everyone?'

She meant his mother, but the words stayed stubbornly in her throat.

'Of course. Archie's a Lao, and soon you will be too.'

She felt a flicker of disappointment, but this wasn't about her. Family mattered—to his father, his sisters, to him—and now she was part of that family.

'I want to do whatever you think is best for the family. That's my priority.'

Something flickered across his eyes, too fast for her to track, much less understand. All she knew was that his smile had faded.

'You're nice, you know…' he said quietly.

He leaned forward, hesitated, and then lowered his mouth to hers and kissed her again—only this kiss was harder, more urgent, as though he was trying to communicate something that was beyond words.

His hands moved over her back, pressing her closer, his fingers sliding beneath the shirt to find hot, bare skin, then lower to the jutting curve of her bottom.

She felt his thigh nudge between hers, parting her legs, and instantly she was melting, arching helplessly against his body, the friction between them making an ache spread out inside her.

He breathed in sharply, breaking the kiss as a light wind rippled across the water, lifting the sails and her hair. She shivered.

'Are you cold?' he asked.

She nodded. 'A little.'

Pulling her closer, he stared down into her eyes and she felt the hard press of his erection. Her body pulsed, aching for him to fill the hollowed-out space inside her.

'Then let's go inside and get warm,' he said softly.

Gazing at his reflection, Charlie frowned. For some reason he could not get the knot of his tie to sit centrally.

'Here, let me.'

He hadn't noticed Dora come into the bathroom. His mind had been somewhere else. But that was as it should be, he told himself.

Today was Qingming. Today was all about the past, about his ancestors. It was about remembering and paying respect to the dead, to his father.

Turning, he stared down at her as she thumbed his tie loose and began patiently re-knotting it.

Her blonde hair was tied back into some kind of chignon, and she was wearing a demure dark fitted dress and black court shoes.

He couldn't fault her appearance.

Qingming was a day of reverence for the dead, and she looked composed and sombre, and yet he couldn't help wishing that she was still lying beside him in bed, wearing her pink-and-white-striped pyjamas. Or, better still, nothing.

'Don't look at me like that,' she said softly.

'Like what?'

Her grey eyes met his, and she bit into her lip. 'You know, like…'

Dropping her gaze, she pulled the knot tight, but he didn't notice. He was too busy looking at the marks on her lip and thinking about how badly he would like to smooth them out with his mouth.

'There—done! Now, can you zip me up?'

Turning away from him, she lowered her head, and he obediently pulled the zip to the top. Staring down at her neck, at the smooth, flawless skin and the tiny, fine down at the hairline, he felt his shoulders tense.

There had been so many times over the last few days when he had wanted to talk to her honestly. To tell her that his feelings had changed. That this relationship was more than just a convenient way for both of them to be a part of Archie's day-to-day life.

That he loved her.

He felt his heart swell at the thought, and that in itself was a shock. To discover that it was not just there to pump blood around his body, but that it beat faster whenever he saw her, held her, heard her voice.

Resting his hands lightly on her shoulders, he pulled her against him, pressing his lips to her hair, breathing in the scent of her warm, clean skin.

I love you.

It was so easy to say it in his head. *Obviously.* In his head he could write a script for Dora to follow. But what he ideally wanted her to say and how she would respond in reality were two different things.

And, in reality, she had no reason to love him.

How could any woman—particularly one as vibrant and uninhibited as Dora—love a man who had nudged her into a loveless marriage?

Revealing his feelings would only lead to a dead end and ruin the closeness and understanding they had found.

His chest tightened. It was ironic that telling the truth would make things more strained and artificial between them.

'The cars are already here,' she said.

He felt her shift, then turn to face him, her grey eyes soft and clear.

'We should probably go downstairs.'

He stared down at her mutely. Now was not the time to tell her how everything felt different all of a sudden.

As usual, his father took precedence.

The journey was unusually quiet. Even Archie seemed to pick on the sombreness of the occasion and sat quietly clasping his monkey in his car seat.

The Lao tomb was noticeably larger and more elaborate than the graves surrounding it. Smoke was drifting across the hillside. Nearby he could hear the sound of firecrackers. The authorities had cracked down on the burning of gifts, but people liked their traditions.

Holding Archie's hand, Charlie swept away the dust and leaves from the tomb. Watching his sisters lay flowers—lilies from Lei, chrysanthemums from Josie and Sabrina—he felt a rush of pity and guilt.

He had been so focused on fulfilling his father's dying wish that he had completely ignored the needs of the living. All that mattered to him was that his sisters *appeared* to be coping.

But surely the point of family was that their ties were not just skin-deep?

Wasn't that what today was about?

Reaching back through generations of family wasn't just a way to remember the dead—it was a reminder of the importance of the living to one another. And that was why people continued to burn gifts and set off firecrackers. To make connections with their loved ones that outlived the smoke and the sparks.

He felt Dora squeeze his hand. 'Are you okay?'

'Yes, I'm fine. Thank you for coming today, and for letting me bring Archie.'

He could hear the distance in his voice even before he saw the hurt in her eyes. He knew he was being unfair. This whole experience was new and alien to her. But, being here, he could almost sense his father's presence, and it was more stifling than the incense and the smoke.

'Let's go home,' he said quietly.

Back at the house, the family made their way through the woods to where the cliffs fell away to the ocean. It was a warm day, but there was a strong breeze.

Perfect kite-flying weather.

'Here.' He handed Dora a beautiful black-and-yellow kite. 'Write down everything you fear on the kite. Everything you dread happening. And then, when the kite is flying, cut the string and your fears will float away in the wind.'

His poetic words made her face soften, as he had known they would, and then her eyes met his.

'Let's do it together,' she said softly.

They let Archie hold the kite. Even though it was tugging at his little hand like an impatient dog, he was strangely calm. His huge dark eyes widened when Charlie cut the string, and then he and Dora gazed up into the sky.

But Charlie didn't watch its final fluttering journey. Instead he was watching them, and thinking about the journey he had made them take.

Acting on his father's wishes, he had brought the two of them here. He had fulfilled his duty as a son against considerable odds and he had united his family, so bringing honour to the Lao name.

He should be feeling immense satisfaction.

But he couldn't shift a sense that in succeeding in one way he had failed in another. And being surrounded by his family today seemed to exacerbate that feeling, so that by the time they had finished eating lunch he was fighting an urge to call Mario so he could work off his pent-up tension in the gym.

Finally everyone left, and Archie went to have a late nap. But now that Charlie and Dora were alone he felt more tense than ever.

'Do you want to go for a swim?' she asked.

He felt her eyes on his face. 'No, I'm not really in the mood.'

Shaking his head, he shifted back against the sofa and tried to stretch out the tightness in his spine.

'Is your back hurting?'

'It's fine. I'm fine.' He frowned. 'I'm sorry, I'm not very good company right now.'

'That's okay.' She bit her lip. 'I can go, if you want.'

'No.' He caught her hand, and the warmth of her skin seemed to stop one thing building in his chest but start another.

'I wish I could do something to help,' she said.

'I can think of something.'

It was a joke—sort of—but it sounded crass and clumsy.

He shook his head. 'Sorry, I don't know why I said that.'

'You're upset.' She hesitated. 'It's okay, Charlie. You don't need to apologise. I do understand.

I know you must miss your father a lot—not just today, but every day. There are so many reminders of him.'

Himself included. He looked down at her hand in his, and some of the tension in his body eased. Dora felt like an antidote. Unlike everyone else in his life, she couldn't hide her feelings.

It wasn't that she didn't try. And to people who didn't know her—people like him, sitting in this house, reading that stupid report—she probably looked as if she didn't care about anything.

Only he knew now that wasn't true. Dora cared a lot. And the way she behaved was the clearest demonstration of that. Not just the self-sabotaging, but the way she sang on stage.

But he had spent so long suppressing and ignoring his feelings that he couldn't even admit them to those closest to him.

Would that be Archie's fate too?

He couldn't imagine it.

His little brother was so elemental, his tears and smiles moving like clouds passing swiftly in front of the sun.

But Charlie must have been like that once. Only that was even harder to imagine.

'Charlie…?'

She was looking at him, uncertainty and concern vying with each other in her face.

'I'm just wondering if you think maybe we should...' she glanced up at his face, not angry, but pensive, a little tense '...if I should meet your mother before the party—you know, in private...'

He heard the hesitation in her voice, the careful way she was phrasing her words to be somewhere between an observation and a question. And, given her relationship to Della, he completely understood her unease.

It would be a daunting enough prospect to come face to face with the wife of your sister's lover. To do so when you were engaged to the woman's son...

But he had been expecting this moment ever since she had agreed to marry him—obviously his mother and his wife could hardly avoid meeting one another. So why, then, had it caught him off guard?

She took a breath. 'It might give us a chance to get past the awkward stuff.'

The awkward stuff.

That was one way of putting it.

He gritted his teeth. The simplest, most obvious response would be to tell her the truth. And he wanted to be honest with her. She had been honest with him, and they had agreed to be honest with one another.

Only as with most truths that had been buried or blurred, it was not simple at all—and in this instance the facts were misleading.

Dora was clearly wondering why he hadn't introduced her to his mother yet. Logically, she assumed that it was because Nuria was upset about the engagement and he didn't want to rush his mother, push her into doing something that would upset her more.

Only that wasn't the reason he was reluctant for them to meet.

He knew Dora would be expecting his mother to be angry—bitter and tearful, even. A part of him suspected that she would almost welcome that kind of reaction.

But even though her husband had cheated on her repeatedly, and fathered an illegitimate child with his mistress, Nuria was still a Lao, and being a Lao came first. And that was why he needed them to meet in public at the party. That way Dora might confuse his mother's composure with a desire not to embarrass her son.

He felt his stomach knot.

It would be fairer, and kinder to Nuria, for them to meet privately, but once again he had to put the needs of the family above her feelings. To do otherwise would raise too many difficult questions.

How could he explain that he had been taught to lie? That being a member of his family required the adoption of a certain code—his father's code—and that meant learning to justify distortion and prevarication.

Family reputation came first. It trumped everything—certainly the petty needs of the individual.

I'm not who you think I am, he wanted to tell Dora.

Only he couldn't unilaterally smash the mirror-gloss perfection of the Lao family…not when so much was riding on it.

After they were married, he would sit down and explain the rules.

And he would do his best to minimise the sacrifices she and Archie would have to make.

Only right now he needed to find a way to answer Dora's question.

He cast around for something to make her accept the situation. 'I think she would find that hard,' he said truthfully. 'It will be easier for her with more people around.'

He felt her flinch, felt it travel through her fingers into his body.

'So that's why she didn't come to the graveyard with us?' she said quietly. 'I'm sorry. That must have been hard for you...not having her there.'

The ache in her voice made his chest tighten with guilt and shame.

His mother had been upset for so long he had barely given it a moment's thought—and then only in regard to the logistics of organising a second limousine. But he was her son as much as his father's and he had let her down—not least because he, not Dora, should have been the one to recognise that simple, immutable truth.

'It's not your fault, it's mine.'

For a moment he pictured his father's lip curling in disdain at his admission. But when he gazed down at Dora his father's features seemed to blur and dwindle like the smoke in the graveyard.

'I handled today badly,' he said. 'I've handled a lot of things badly. Got my priorities wrong. Let down the people who need me most. But I want that to stop now.'

He meant it; he wanted to break the cycle and give Dora and Archie a different kind of life—a life that wouldn't require the forfeiture of their own hopes and needs.

But the truth was that once he married Dora she and Archie—like him and his sisters and his mother and his stepmothers—would disappear beneath the faultless façade of his family.

CHAPTER TEN

NOTHING—NO NUMBER of Rolls-Royces, designer dresses and private yachts—could have prepared her for this, Dora thought, looking over at the glittering guests filling the vast reception room at the Black Tiger. Charlie had been right. Parties really were his sisters' thing.

Back in London she had been to a handful of engagement parties and most had been modest affairs, with friends and family toasting the happy couple with a glass of supermarket Prosecco.

This, though, was grander and more opulent by far.

Smoky grey chesterfields and wicker furniture flanked the dance floor, and the original nineteen-twenties café-style tables were heaving with pale apricot-coloured roses.

One thousand guests had dined on *toro tartare* with caviar, dim sum, and peach granita dusted with silver leaf.

Now uniformed waiters wove between them with trays of vintage champagne and bellinis while they listened and danced to the jazz band playing Cole Porter and Gershwin.

Dora gazed over at the band, a smile pulling at her mouth. They were excellent, their harmonies taking you irresistibly back to a different, more glamorous age, but without tipping over into the kind of lazy nostalgia she loathed.

'What's the verdict?'

Charlie. Breathing in, she braced herself against the wave of emotions both painful and pleasurable that accompanied looking at him.

'They're amazing.' She smiled up at him, then glanced across the room. 'It's all amazing.'

'*You're* amazing,' he said quietly. His dark eyes roamed appreciatively over her smoky-grey georgette dress. 'You look like a movie star.'

'Your sisters have impeccable taste,' she said lightly.

'Their brother does too.'

The corners of his mouth pulled into the kind of smile that made heat burrow down through her body.

'You look like a movie star,' she echoed, reaching out to touch the lapel of his dark suit.

Actually, he looked like danger and power and

beauty. No wonder everyone was falling over themselves to talk to him.

Or that she had fallen head over heels in love with him.

Her smile slipped a little and, blanking her mind, she pasted it back on her face.

It felt odd, pushing her love for him away at their engagement party, but she had done this so many times before—let hope and possibilities flood her head—and she knew the more she let it build the more it would hurt to watch it drain away.

'Dora—Archie grabbed my drink and he's got all wet.'

Lei was standing beside them, holding Archie. She was wearing a black rose-smothered silk dress and she looked flawlessly beautiful, and perhaps it was because of that flawlessness that Dora noticed the slight tension in her voice.

'I'll change him,' she said.

'I'll get Shengyi.' Charlie glanced over his shoulder to where the nanny was hovering discreetly.

But Archie had seen Dora and was already reaching out to her.

'It's fine, I can do—'

She came to a stop, silenced by the flicker of longing in the other woman's eyes.

'Actually, Lei…could you help me?'

A room had been set aside for Archie, and they headed there. Lying him down on the changing table, Dora began unbuttoning his dungarees.

'You are such a mucky monkey. Now, lie still while your big sister Lei gets you dressed.'

Heart leaping, she watched as Lei gently changed him into a clean top and shorts. It was none of Dora's business, but she had learned from experience that it was misguided and ultimately pointless pretending that something was okay when it wasn't.

'How long have you been trying?' she asked quietly.

She felt rather than saw Lei flinch, and knew that she had said too much.

'Nearly two years. There's nothing wrong. We've had tests.'

The flatness in the other woman's voice made her heart contract. It reminded her of how Della had sounded: defeated and sad.

'I don't know what I'd do if it was me. Probably give up.' She gave Lei a small, tight smile. 'I'm not brave, like you. You're fighting for what you want, and that means you *will* get a baby—

somehow, some way. And in the meantime you can practise with Archie.'

Lei was staring at her. 'My brother is lucky to have you.'

Dora felt her skin grow tight. She knew her face was flushed—knew too that she wanted to confide in Lei as she would have done with Della. But honesty was not the best policy here.

'And Archie is lucky to have you,' she said.

'Lei.' It was her husband, Thomas. 'Your mother is here.'

And just like that the intimacy between them was gone and the guard was back up. 'I should go.'

Dora nodded. 'Yes, go. I'll be out in a second.'

Their eyes met and then Lei was gone. Dora heard the door close and, needing to shift the tightness in her throat, she picked Archie up and kissed his neck, making him squirm and giggle.

'He looks like Charlie did at that age.'

Startled, Dora spun round and felt her stomach drop.

Nuria Rivero hadn't arrived by the time she and Lei had slipped away from the party, but she was here now.

Dora swallowed—or rather tried to swallow past the panic swelling in her throat.

'I hope you don't mind me intruding, Dora. I just wanted to meet the woman who is going to marry my son, but privately, without all the fuss.'

She had a beautiful voice, Dora thought. Soft, husky, with just the faintest hint of an accent. In fact, she was a very beautiful woman. Petite and slim, with shining dark hair and green eyes, and the same high cheekbones and curving mouth as Charlie.

'Of course.' She nodded, feeling suddenly ashamed that of all the people here this woman had been forced to seek her out.

Nuria walked across the room and stopped in front of her. 'And this must be Archie. How old is he now?'

'He's one.'

'Such a lovely age.'

Reaching out, Nuria touched Archie's hand. Instantly he grabbed her finger and began to squeeze it tightly, giggling.

'Look at that face. He's beautiful. You must love him so much.'

Dora nodded. But she wasn't looking at Archie's face. Instead she was looking at the other woman. There was no doubt about it; Nuria had been crying.

It wouldn't be noticeable to most people, Dora

thought, her stomach twisting, but she knew the signs. Extra blusher to distract from the redness around the eyes. Retouched mascara. And a smile that looked ever so slightly forced.

Dora felt sick. This was the flipside of Della's affair. This devastated woman who had carefully made up her face so that she could go to her son's engagement party.

Her eyes felt hot. She was out of her depth. Her sister had taken Nuria's husband. Now Dora was taking her son. What could she possibly say that would in any way make up for that?

'I'm sorry,' she whispered. 'I'm so sorry for what Della did. I know you probably won't believe me, but she never wanted to hurt you. And she didn't plan to get pregnant.'

'I'm sorry too.' Nuria smiled at her sadly, her irises suddenly very green. 'Sorry for what my husband did...what I let him do.'

'It wasn't your fault.'

'Do you love my son?' The older woman was suddenly fighting to speak. 'Do you love Charlie?'

Dora felt her heart swell. Always, before she had met Charlie, she had been scared. Scared to trust, scared of hoping to find her place in the world, and most of all she had been scared to love.

She had hidden those fears from everyone except her sister, but then she had met Charlie, and he had pulled her close even as she was pushing him away, held her and comforted her and made her see that she mattered, that she had always mattered.

'I didn't want to,' she said slowly. 'Not at first. In fact, I hated him.'

Shivering, she thought back to that first time they'd met. She knew now that it hadn't been hate she had felt, but fear—fear of that irresistible pull between them and the knowledge that what she was feeling would mean giving away a part of herself for ever.

And she had done it anyway.

'Only then I got to know him and now I love him. Like I loved Della...like I love Archie.'

Was she making it clear enough? If only she could sing it, she thought with a wrench.

'I don't know how to describe it except that when I'm with him I don't want that day to end, and every morning when I wake up I can't wait to spend another day with him.'

'And he feels the same way,' Nuria said softly. 'He's not been raised to show his feelings, but—'

her voice broke a little '—but I know my son, and he loves you very much.'

Dora stared at her in silence, struggling to breathe, let alone speak, wanting to believe her words.

But Nuria was Charlie's mother—she saw what she wanted to see. And why would she think that her son was marrying for anything other than love?

Dora's hands tightened around Archie. She could end this now. Stop the lies and the guilt filling her chest like a dark cloud. But how could she tell Charlie's mother than her son had never and would never love her?

Nuria looked her directly in the eye. 'So please, please, do a better job of protecting him than I did.'

'There you are. I've been looking for you—'

She and Nuria turned as one. It was Charlie.

His dark eyes moved from Dora's face to his mother's. 'Everything okay?' he asked slowly.

Dora blinked. She had just told his mother that she loved him, and more than anything she wanted to tell Charlie too. But she had already given away so much to him that she would never get back.

'Everything's fine. I'm going to take Archie

back out to the party now. Don't forget we're making the announcement at three.'

Charlie watched as Dora slipped through the door. His heart was pounding. He felt dizzy, confused. Introducing Dora to his mother had felt like the biggest deal inside his head. He had told so many lies, had so many regrets.

Only now it had happened—and without him.

'Charlie—'

He stared down at his mother, not only seeing the tears in her eyes but for the first time acknowledging them. What must it have felt like for her? To be told that her son was marrying this particular woman; to know she'd have to meet her husband's love child.

And that was just today. What about everything that had gone before?

Yes, she had played her part in the distance that had come between them—willingly at first, and then with increasing reluctance. But he didn't know what was more tragic: that she should have walled herself away from her son or that he had let her do so.

Reaching out, he took her hand and held it against his cheek. 'I know how hard this is for

you. All of this,' he said slowly. 'And I'm sorry...
so sorry that I haven't done more—'

'Shh...' Shaking her head, his mother pressed
her finger against his mouth. 'I know—I know,
querido, but it can wait, Charlie.' She gave him a
watery smile. 'Let's not worry about what can't
be changed. Today I want to hear about the future. Now, tell me, have you chosen a date for
the wedding?'

He nodded, letting her lead him away from the
damage of the past.

'September the third seems the most auspi-
cious date.'

'That's good—although I think fortune is already on your side.' His mother's beautiful green
eyes found his. 'Now the whole family will be together, and I know how important that is to you.'

'To you too—to all of us.' He forced himself
to hold her gaze.

'And that's it? That's the reason you're marrying Dora? To bring Archie home to the family?'

'Yes,' he said quietly.

'I don't believe you.' Her eyes were bright with
the sheen of tears. 'I know you love her.'

'No—' He tried to shake his head, but his body
felt suddenly leaden. 'I can't love her. I don't
know how to love.'

'Yes, you can. You do. And Dora loves you too.'

His chin jerked up, disbelief and hope briefly displacing the misery in his chest. But of course his mother was wrong.

You know how this works, he wanted to say. *You're still making it work.*

'She doesn't love me. She's marrying me for Archie's sake. To give him access to all this.' He couldn't keep the bitterness out of his voice.

His mother smiled at him sadly. 'She loves you, Charlie. Really loves you. Your father never loved me. He wanted me, but he only married me after he found out you were a boy.' She was suddenly struggling to speak. 'I should have divorced him years ago. But I was too cowardly, and weak. My weakness hurt you, and I'm sorry I wasn't stronger for you.'

The pain and sadness in her face felt like a blade against his heart. 'You were very young and you did your best.'

She shook her head. 'I was young, and I was frightened of being alone. I told myself I was doing it out of love for you, and that was true.'

His eyes were prickling. Her love for him was indisputable, as was his for her. 'I know,' he said hoarsely.

'But love should be about giving as well as

taking.' Her hand tightened around his. 'You're a good man, Charlie; now's your chance to be a better one.'

Walking back into the Black Tiger's huge reception room, Charlie felt as though he might stumble. Everything was so perfect, so flawless, as every Lao function always was. It looked like a film set.

Except this wasn't a film. It was real life. With real people, not actors. And their smiles and tears were real too—or they were supposed to be.

His heart contracted as he spotted Dora's blonde hair across the room. She was standing with his sisters, Archie in her arms.

Seeing her with his mother, he had felt a rush of agonising emotions. Hope, remorse, and, more than anything, fear. And now that fear was rising up inside him, more dark and terrible than any dragon.

Could Dora love him? He wanted it to be true, more than he had ever wanted anything, and yet...

His fingers brushed against hers, and she glanced up at him, her soft grey eyes searching his face with an eagerness and concern that made his heart pound. And then Arnaldo was beside him with a microphone and he was turning towards the guests.

'Good afternoon, everyone. Thank you for coming here today. It's wonderful to see you all.' He paused, picturing his father's face, the gleam of approval that he had spent half his life chasing. 'As you know, I have an announcement to make...'

He caught a glimpse of his sisters' faces. As ever, they were glossily perfect, and normally he would have looked away at that point. But today his eyes were drawn to the tension in Lei's shoulders, the downward tilt of Josie's mouth and Sabrina's over-bright smile.

He felt a rush of panic. His sisters were all acting their parts, but now, as never before, it hurt to see it. Hurt to think of the women they might have become.

His gaze drifted to where his mother stood, beside his father's other wives. It hurt more to think of the women they would become.

Love should be about giving, not just taking. *Be a better man*—that was what his mother had said. And what better time to start than now, here?

He glanced over at Dora. She would give everything to love. She would do it for Archie, for him. But life had already taken more from her than it had given and, loving her like he did, he couldn't bear to strip her of everything he loved about her: her impulsiveness, her spark of defiance, her candour.

He handed the microphone back to Arnaldo and turned towards her. 'I'm sorry,' he said softly, and then, ignoring the murmur rising up around him, he spun round and walked away.

Dora gazed after him in shock. She felt Archie shift against her, his eyes following Charlie out of the room.

Around her the guests were turning to one another, their voices low but their confusion audible. It was a sound she recognised—one that was imprinted on her brain from that night in the club.

It was suddenly difficult to breathe. He had left her. Charlie had left her. She felt her body start to fill with a jagged sadness that blotted out everything, even the muscular panic squeezing her throat.

For a moment she couldn't move, couldn't think or even see, and then slowly faces came into focus. Lei's face. Nuria's face. And with them came words—Della's words, from what felt like another lifetime.

'I wish I'd done more, Dora. To fight for him, to fight for us. Whatever the outcome, I should have done that.'

Turning to Lei, she pushed Archie into her arms. 'Look after him for me.'

'Take as long as you want.' Lei's eyes met hers. 'As long as you need.'

Lifting up the hem of her dress, Dora walked swiftly between the clumps of guests. In the foyer, there was no sign of Charlie and, taking a deep breath, she turned in a circle. And then suddenly she knew where he would be and, heart beating hard, she began moving more quickly.

The boat felt like the *Marie Celeste* and, listening to the dull slap of waves against the hull, she worried that she had got it wrong.

And then she saw him.

He was leaning against the handrail, gazing out across the ocean, and something in the stretch of his shoulders made her square her own.

He turned, and the expression on his face almost made her resolve falter.

'Charlie—' she began.

He shook his head. 'It's over, Dora.'

'It is not over.' She stopped in front of him, her heart hammering against her ribs. 'It's not over because I love you.'

'I know.' His eyes found hers. 'And I love you. But that's why it has to end now.'

Now it was her turn to shake her head. 'You're not making any sense.'

'Only because you don't understand what's going on here.'

He looked away, his face tightening, as if it hurt to say the words out loud.

'So tell me, then.'

Charlie looked down at her wide, determined eyes, his chest aching.

'Do you remember when I had the stylist send over those dresses? You got upset. You said they were worth more than your salary.'

'I remember,' she said quietly. 'And you said that was what being a Lao meant.'

'I did—but I lied. Being a Lao means putting the family above yourself. We do whatever it takes, make any sacrifice. It has to look perfect. That's the price you pay for admission. I don't want that for you, and I don't want that for Archie. You deserve better—you both do.'

'So do you.'

The ache in his chest was spreading. It was a gaping wound now.

'No, I don't. I'm not a good man. I've spent my life putting business and power before everything else, and particularly my family. My sisters, my mother—'

He couldn't risk influencing Archie. Damaging him.

'Why did you do that?'

There was no judgement in her voice and, meeting her gaze, he saw that there was no judgement there either.

'My mother was his mistress. He never loved her. She was too needy, too emotional. He wouldn't marry her—not even when he found out she was pregnant.' His mouth twisted. 'But then he found out I was a boy and I think he let his ego, the idea of having his name pass down the generations, overrule his reason.'

'What happened?'

He shrugged. 'He divorced Ina—that's Josie and Sabrina's mother—and married my mother. But she was terrified of losing him. You know what they say. When a man marries his mistress—'

'There's a vacancy.'

He nodded. 'They stayed married, but they basically lived separate lives from when I was about three.' His eyes met hers. 'There were compensations. He gave her a beautiful home, made sure she had no financial worries. All she had to do was show up and smile and play the loving wife.'

Dora breathed out shakily. His mother had acted a part out of fear and desperation, with Charlie not much older than Archie. How much had he absorbed? Had he felt responsible? Blamed himself?

Looking up at his face, she didn't need to ask.

'And she had to let him teach me how to become a worthy successor and heir to the throne.' His mouth twisted. 'I might have lived with her, but he had expectations—"requirements" of his son—so she basically let him bring me up, even though it broke her heart. Mine too.'

Dora felt sick. So that was why Nuria had asked her to do a better job of protecting him.

'It didn't make any difference,' he said slowly. 'He was discreet, but he was never faithful to her—though he *was* careful not to make the same mistake again. Until Della… Sorry.' He frowned. 'I didn't mean she was a mistake. Or Archie.'

Watching his face, Dora felt as though her heart would break. He looked so miserable, so exactly the way she had used to feel.

Reaching out, she found his hands. 'That's okay.'

'No, it's not. I was scared of ending up like my mother, like my sisters, their mothers, and it made me selfish. But everyone was disposable to my father.'

His voice was level, but that only seemed to make what he was saying seem more brutal.

'Even being his child felt more like a goal than a right.'

'Nobody's son,' she said softly.

'I have a mother. I just didn't let her be one.'

'There's still time.'

Charlie was shocked by the force of hope he felt at her words. 'I don't want to be my father.'

'Charlie, you just walked out of your engagement party. In front of a thousand people. Without caring what they think.' She breathed out shakily. 'I don't think you need to worry about that.'

He started to laugh, and she smiled, and then he felt his body begin to shake as he realised how close he had come to losing her and Archie. He pulled her against him, pressing her close, and the steady beat of her heart was like the first drops of rain after a long, dry summer.

'I've never talked like this to anyone,' he said slowly. 'You've changed me, Dora Thorn. When I met you I was unreachable. I'd forgotten who I was, who I wanted to be, and you found me.'

'You changed me too. If I hadn't met you I would never have been able to come after you. You made me let go of my fears.'

His dark eyes rested on her face. 'So do you think that's a good enough reason to get married?'

'It's okay—but I've got a better one.'

'What's that?' he asked softly.

'I love you and you love me.'

'Isn't that two reasons?'

She bit into the smile curving her mouth. 'That's why you're in charge of the casino and I'm in charge of entertainment.'

He smiled. 'Is Archie okay? Do you think we should go back to the party?'

'Lei's got him.' She hesitated. 'And she did say we could take as long as we needed.'

'In that case, I think the party can wait. From now on I'm putting you first.'

And, ignoring her yelp of surprise, he scooped her up into his arms and carried her down to the cabin.

EPILOGUE

GAZING DOWN AT the piano keyboard, Dora frowned. She played a couple of notes softly. It was early, and she didn't want to wake Charlie. Hesitating, she played them again, changing them slightly, then replayed the first version and sang a couple of bars, testing the rhythm, feeling her way through the chords.

That was it, she thought, a ripple of happiness running over her skin.

It was still so new, so incredible to her. But amazingly—unbelievably—her voice had returned.

At first it had been just a shift in feeling—a slow but fluid sense of having something reawakening inside her. And then it had been impossible to hold back…like floodwater pushing through a levee.

But that wasn't the only change to her life.

Looking down at the slim gold band on her finger, she felt her heartbeat stumble.

She and Charlie had married four months ago and this beautiful piano had been his present to her, a wedding day gift—not that she had needed or wanted anything but him.

He was her heart, her soul, her love. And he felt the same way.

He was no longer the man who had dragged her across the ocean to prove her frailties. Now he loved her as she loved him—completely and unconditionally.

It had been a simple private ceremony, on a clear, bright morning. Few guests, no press. Just his mother, his sisters and their partners, and of course Archie.

Her eyes felt suddenly hot.

It wasn't just she and Charlie who had changed. Archie had changed too. He still got cross, but now they were the usual toddler tantrums about having to wear his coat or wanting to eat pudding first.

The alternately angry and then clingy baby was gone. He felt safe. His life was stable now, and it showed. He was a normal, happy little boy.

Pressing the damper pedal down again, she played the song, feeling the notes vibrate through her body as she remembered the last few months in her head.

Charlie had insisted that they both have bereavement counselling, and it had helped her understand the process of grieving: the guilt, the anger, the despair and finally the acceptance.

But accepting that Della was gone didn't mean that she would ever forget her sister. She couldn't—Della was in every cell of her body. Archie's too.

And he was so like Della: serious and focused and super-bright. But when he smiled, her heart melted.

Just like it did with his brother.

She didn't need to look in a mirror to know that she had a big, stupid smile on her face. Even thinking about him made a fluttering happiness rise up inside of her like migrating butterflies.

She had never been so happy—hadn't known that this kind of happiness existed, hadn't known that it was possible to love and be loved like this.

She felt as if a flame had been lit inside her. A flame that had burned away all her fears and doubts about herself.

Charlie had looked inside her and he'd liked what he saw.

Really, really liked it.

Remembering the hard urgency of his mouth and the light, teasing touch of his hands on her skin, she felt her breath shorten. He liked what he saw on the outside too.

Releasing the pedal, she leaned into the keyboard and, opening her mouth, sang from her heart—sang the song as she had written it to be sung.

As the last note faded to silence she heard a slow, steady hand-clap and, turning on the piano stool, she felt her stomach flip over.

Charlie was leaning against the door frame, his dark eyes resting on her face. He was wearing loose cotton pyjama bottoms and his hair was flopping across his forehead in the same way it did when he rolled her body beneath his in their bed upstairs.

Her heart began beating faster. He was so mesmerisingly beautiful that every time she saw him she had the same feeling of not being able to look away. But it wasn't just his looks that drew her to him. Charlie made her feel as though every day was the first day of spring. Just being with him made her think of warmer days and soft green leaves—and new life.

'You should have woken me.'

'You were sleeping.'

He held her gaze. 'Was that the song you've been working on?'

She nodded. 'It came together this morning.'

His mouth curved into a slow smile that made heat rise up inside her. 'Yes, it did,' he said softly.

Watching the flush of colour rise over her cheeks, Charlie walked across the room towards her, but she was already moving towards him.

They met halfway, her lips finding his as his arms curled around her body.

He wasn't sure this feeling would ever go away—this feeling of wanting to hold her close—or the way her nearness and the soft beat of her heart warmed him.

Seeing her at the piano, hearing her sing, made something tear inside him. He knew how much it meant to her, so it meant everything to him.

Burying his face in her hair, he breathed in her scent, feeling blessed. Grateful. Whole.

So much had changed since that day when she had come after him. He was going to a counsellor and now, thanks to Dora, he could talk about himself, reveal the hurt and the loneliness of those years he'd spent trying to meet his father's demands.

Miraculously—and again thanks to Dora—he had grown closer to his mother and his sisters too. It wasn't easy—there were still days when he found it hard to forget the need to pretend, to protect himself, to keep his distance—but Dora and Archie, and his mother and his sisters, needed him to be whole. And his father's way would stop him from being the man, the husband, the brother, the son they needed.

Being honest with himself, with his family, was hard, but he knew now that it was necessary for the life he wanted and needed to live.

'You're not missing him too much, are you?' he asked softly.

They had left Archie with Nuria. His chest tightened as he remembered how thrilled his mother had been when they'd asked her to take care of him. She was so excited—touchingly so—to be an *Avó*, and she adored Archie.

His sisters doted on him too, and now that Lei had found out she was pregnant she was at the house most days, practising her 'mummy' skills.

'I do miss him, but I know he's fine. And, anyway, I wanted it to be just the two of us.'

He nodded, his heart contracting with the love he was learning to express more with every passing day.

'I want that too.' Pressing her against him, he kissed her slowly, hungrily, the soft hitch of her breath making his body harden with unqualified speed.

'We need to make the most of it. I mean, it might be the last chance we get for a bit,' she said softly. 'When the baby arrives we won't have much time to ourselves.'

His gaze drifted over her vest and cropped denim shorts, lingering on the bare skin of her throat and thighs. 'I think we have time. Lei isn't due until the New Year.'

She gazed up at him, her grey eyes hazy with a love that mirrored his own, and then, taking his hand, she rested it gently against her belly. 'I wasn't talking about Lei's baby.'

His face stilled. 'You're having a baby?'

He was stunned.

Drawing a deep breath, she nodded. 'I'm having *our* baby.'

'Our baby…'

They could both hear the choke in his voice as he smiled, his eyes full of tears of happiness.

'Yes, our baby. We're a family now,' she said softly.

And he pulled closer, kissing her with tenderness and passion as sunlight began filling the room.

* * * * *

LET'S TALK
Romance

For exclusive extracts, competitions
and special offers, find us online:

�f facebook.com/millsandboon

📷 @millsandboonuk

🐦 @millsandboon

Or get in touch on 0844 844 1351*

For all the latest titles coming soon,
visit millsandboon.co.uk/nextmonth

*Calls cost 7p per minute plus your phone company's price per
minute access charge